Identity Crisis

By Charles Huss

For my wife, Rose, who always believed in me more than I believed in myself.

Introduction

The beginning of my incredible story started when something potentially life-changing was revealed to me, but before my life could be changed, something else occurred that would have a profound impact on my future in ways I could never have imagined. This is my story.

Chapter 1

It was a Friday evening in early March. I don't remember the date, but it felt like summer as I left work. At the time, I worked in the IT department for a large financial institution in Tampa. I was one of the computer geeks that kept the place running.

After the long drive home, I was tired and irritable when my wife, Lisa, met me at the door. She was wearing a beautiful, low-cut red dress that seemed designed to show off her perfect curves. The dress was knee-length with a slit up the left side that showed off her long, smooth legs. The whole thing was held up by two thin straps that looked like they would break at any sudden movement. I remembered the dress. She had worn it three months earlier at the rehearsal dinner the day before our wedding.

She kissed me and said, "Welcome home, baby." Her long, silky blonde hair fell over her shoulders as she turned to lead me toward the dining room, where she had the table set with the fine china that her parents had given us for our wedding. She had two candles burning near the center of the table and ice water in fancy glasses. I didn't see any wine, though.

"What's the occasion?" I said as I desperately tried to think if I had forgotten some important date. "It's not our anniversary. I know it took me a long time to get home, but not nine months."

"Have a seat, Silly," she said as she disappeared into the kitchen. This was quite a surprise because Lisa was not much of a cook. She taught fifth grade at our local elementary school and would often work on lesson plans or grading homework after school, and we would end up ordering takeout or we would put a frozen pizza in the oven for dinner.

She came back with a bag and started taking out Chinese food containers. "You are too funny," I said.

She laughed and said, "This is the fanciest dinner you will probably ever see in this house, so enjoy it."

"I'm fine with that," I said as I sat down, "but I would like to know what the occasion is?"

"Well, I guess I should just come out with it," Lisa said. "I'm pregnant."

She studied my face for a reaction. I probably should have been more surprised, but I think a part of me was expecting it. We did talk about having children, and while we were not actively trying, we were also not actively not trying. "That's fantastic," I said. "I mean, it's a little scary, but I really am very happy."

"Really?" she said, smiling. "I was worried that the news might freak you out somewhat."

"Really," I said and got up and hugged her. "I will admit that I'm concerned about my ability to be a good father. I mean, I know nothing about raising children, but I know for certain that you are going to make a wonderful mother. That fact alone makes me feel better because I know you will make up for my inadequacies."

"Relax, you'll be fine," she said. "Nobody knows how to be a parent before their first child is born. By the time their second child arrives, they are old pros."

"Second child?"

"Let's just take this one child at a time," she said. "Hey, we should tell your dad."

"Okay, I'll call him after dinner."

"You can't call your father with news like this. We have to tell him in person."

"Honey, you know that's not going to happen without a week's notice," I said. "Since Mom died, he is always working. Why don't we tell your parents?"

"I already did. Sorry, but I couldn't wait."

"That's fine. Your parents are always there for you. My father is a different story."

"Despite what you might think, your father is a good man."

Lisa and Dad always got along well, and it sometimes seemed like she was as much his daughter as I was his son. Before our wedding, I joked that he should like her less so I wouldn't feel like I was about to marry my sister.

Mom liked Lisa too when she could remember who she was. She was diagnosed with early-onset Alzheimer's disease while I was away at college. I met Lisa in my first year at college and brought her home with me during Christmas break. At that time, Mom was a bit more forgetful than usual, but I would not find out there was something wrong with her until the following spring.

"Tomorrow's Saturday," she said. "Call him and tell him we want to come and see him."

"Okay, I'll call him after dinner, but he will probably be busy."

When I called Dad, he was happy we wanted to visit him, but he had just made a breakthrough at work and planned to go in over the weekend to conduct more experiments. "Why don't you come to the lab tomorrow?" he said. "We can talk there, and I can show you what we are working on."

"I guess we could do that," I said. "How does 10:30 sound?" I figured Lisa and I could stop for breakfast on the way since it was doubtful dad would want to take time to eat.

"That's perfect," he said. "I'll see you then."

When I hung up the phone, it occurred to me that he hadn't sounded that happy in ages. I wondered what got him so excited.

Chapter 2

Dad had been a well-respected neurologist ever since I could remember, which was ironic considering my mother's illness. Shortly after her diagnosis, Dad accepted a position as Professor of Neuroscience at West Florida University in Tampa. He thought the better hours would give him more time to be with Mom. He also had access to their research laboratory, which he hoped to use to find a treatment for Mom's condition. Unfortunately, Dad never found the treatment he was looking for, and Mom passed away four years later.

We arrived at Dad's office five minutes early. His office door had a large window at the top. Under the window was a nameplate that read "Dr. Bernard Neumann." The window had a blind that was closed, but it was still obvious that the lights were not on. I tried the door, but it was locked.

"Wouldn't you know it?" I said.

"We are early," Lisa said. "Let's give him a few minutes."

We heard footsteps and turned to see a very tall black man walking toward us. He was about six and a half feet tall but probably weighed less than I did in high school. I recognized him as a friend and coworker of my dad, Dr. William Patterson. I always called him "Dr. Bill." When Dad graduated medical school and became a resident, Dr. Bill was his attending physician. Dr. Bill was the one who talked Dad into taking the job at the university. He was in his mid-sixties with a receding hairline but not a grey hair on his head. He always seemed to be smiling, as he was doing now. That's probably why Dad liked him.

"Good morning, Dr. Bill," I said. "I see you are still on your hunger strike."

He laughed loudly and said, "You certainly are your father's son." He turned his attention to Lisa and said, "Lisa, it is so good to see you again. You look as beautiful today as you did on your wedding day."

I noticed a slight blush on Lisa's face, and she said, "Thank you so much, Dr. Patterson."

"Please, call me Bill," he said. He looked at me and added, "Your father is in the lab. He asked me to find you. Have you been to the lab before?"

"No, we haven't," I said.

"I'll show you where it is," he said, "Follow me."

He led us to the elevator, and we went inside. He held his ID badge against a sensor and hit the button for the third floor. We got off the elevator, and I noticed a large sign that said, "Research - Authorized Personnel Only." It surprised me that a school would be so restrictive, but I guessed any patents they obtained were of value to the school, and they needed to protect their research.

We turned left and entered a long hallway with doors on both sides. Every thirty feet or so, there was another set of doors. I guessed there were about a dozen rooms but didn't count them. We stopped at the second door on the left. The sign said, "Neurology Lab." Dr. Bill pushed the door open and motioned us inside. He said, "I have a lot of work that I must catch up on, so I'm going back to my office. It was nice seeing both of you again." We smiled and thanked him before going inside.

As we entered the lab, I noticed it was about the size of a high school classroom. The left wall looked like a kitchen. It had a long countertop with cabinets above and below and a sink in the middle. On the far wall were three large storage cabinets. Next to them were several rolling carts with what looked like medical equipment. Along the right wall was a long bench separated into four small workstations with a stool in front of each section. It made me think of Santa's workshop. What looked like a large metal donut was in the middle of the room. I assumed it was one of those open MRI machines, but I wasn't sure. Next to the machine were three workstations, each with at least two computer monitors. It was quiet except for a slight hum that seemed to be coming from all around us.

The room was empty of people except for a young man at one of the workstations and my father standing behind him, looking at the monitors. When he saw us, he stood up straight, smiled, and said, "Alex! Lisa! I'm so glad you could come. I'll be just a second." He turned back to look at the monitors again and said something to the young man. He looked at us and said, "You're just in time. We need a couple more test subjects."

"Test subjects?" I said. "You're joking, right?"

"We just made a breakthrough, Alex. We need more data to confirm our results. Perhaps you and Lisa could help us out."

"We're not guinea pigs, Dad. Don't you have minions for that?"

"If by minions you mean students, then the answer is no. I only have minions Monday through Friday, except Jason here," he said jokingly as he patted Jason on the shoulder. "It's perfectly safe. Jason and I did it already. We need a couple more scans for comparison."

"Scans?" I asked. "You mean using that MRI thingy?"

"It's significantly more advanced than an MRI machine, but it is similar," Dad said. "We'll just take a simple brain scan. There's no danger to you, and you'd be helping us out."

"We came here to tell you something important, Dad."

"Twenty minutes, tops, for both of you. Then we can go out for lunch. My treat."

I looked over at Lisa, who looked back at me and shrugged. "Okay," I said. "What do you want us to do?"

Dad instructed me to lie face up on a table connected to the brain-scanning machine with my head toward the donut. I couldn't see what was happening, but I did hear tapping on the keyboard. The machine kicked on, and it started to make a somewhat loud banging noise. I was worried it was about to self-destruct, but I heard Dad say, "Keep perfectly still, Alex. This will only take a couple of minutes."

Suddenly the table started to move me toward the machine. I slowly entered the donut. Everything was very well-lit, but there wasn't much to see. Then everything went dark.

Chapter 3

After what seemed like only a few seconds, the light returned. I felt different, like I was waking up from a dream. I opened my eyes and saw what looked like a hospital room, but everything was slightly blurry. To my left was a woman, maybe in her early forties, wearing a lab coat and looking at a small tablet computer. She was thin, perhaps a little taller than average. Her hair was dark, but she did have a few thin grey streaks. She had her hair tied behind her head in a bun. I tried to read her name tag, but my eyes had not yet fully focused. It looked like it said, "Dr. Cam."

To the doctor's right was a man wearing a three-piece suit. He was of average height but seemed to be in good shape. His suit couldn't hide that he was obviously into physical fitness. He looked slightly younger than the doctor, perhaps in his late thirties, with dark hair and a handsome, chiseled face. For a moment, I thought he might be an actor, and I was on some weird reality show.

Next to him was a man wearing an Army uniform. He had straight, dark hair with a little grey at the temples. He reminded me a little of Pierce Bronson but shorter and younger. I noticed he had two stars on his shoulders. I have never been in the military, but I was pretty sure that meant he was a Major General, which was surprising because he seemed young for that rank. The fact that he was there made me even more concerned. If this wasn't a joke, I was in the middle of something very serious.

The doctor spoke first. "Welcome back, Mr. Neumann," she said. "I'm Doctor Carr. How are you feeling?"

"I feel fine," I said, my voice a bit hoarse. "Where am I? What happened?" Whatever was happening felt very weird. It seemed like only a few minutes had passed since I was in my father's lab, but I was indeed out for a while. If I was unconscious, why didn't I dream? Do unconscious people dream? Maybe being in Dad's lab was a dream, or perhaps I was dreaming now. All these thoughts were running through my head.

"Hello, Alex," interrupted the man. "My name is Scott Parker. I run this facility. This is General Brian Rafferty. We have a lot to tell you, but much of it is sensitive information. I will tell you all I can, but first, the good doctor needs to monitor you for a while to ensure you are okay. I will come back soon." With that, he turned and walked out the door. The general paused for a second or two and then followed Parker out the door.

I tried to sit up but couldn't and realized I was strapped to the bed. "What the hell is going on here? Am I a prisoner?"

"Please relax, Mr. Neumann," the doctor said. "You have several sensors attached to your body, and the straps keep you from accidentally removing them. Please lie still for about ten minutes. That should give me enough data, and then we can unhook you and let you stretch your muscles."

"Fine," I said. "It's not like I have much choice."

She smiled warmly and said, "I'll be back in a few minutes." When she walked out, I saw a man standing outside the door. He was wearing a uniform, like a security guard.

Several minutes later, Dr. Carr, Scott Parker, and the general returned to the room together. The doctor looked at her equipment and pulled the sheet to uncover my bare chest. "We'll have you out of this in just a minute," she said as she pulled the sensors off me. She then pulled the sheet back up and walked toward the door.

"Wait," I said, "what about the straps?"

She stopped briefly but, without looking back, continued out the door.

"I will take care of that, Mr. Neumann," Parker said, "but first, I need to discuss a few things with you."

"What things?" I asked.

General Rafferty said, "What we are about to tell you is top secret. You cannot divulge anything you learn here to anyone, and I mean anyone. Doing so could be considered an act of treason. Do you understand?"

"I understand," I said, even though I didn't understand. The whole thing seemed like a dream, but it was more like a nightmare.

"My company is called 'Parker Biosystems,'" Parker said. "We contract almost exclusively with certain branches of the government, mostly the military. Our specialty is in integrating technology with human biology. I can't talk about most of what we do here, but some things are no longer classified. You may have read about paraplegics who can spell words using their minds. We developed a similar technology for the Air Force that allows pilots to control their aircraft using just their thoughts. That may not seem like it would make much difference, but the split-second delay between thought and action could be the difference between life and death for a fighter pilot."

"That's all fascinating, Mr. Parker, but what does that have to do with me?"

"Well, manipulating machines using the mind eventually led us to think about the reverse. What if we could change the mind using a machine? At about this time, we heard about your father's invention."

"An invention he never got a chance to tell me about," I said.

"Oh, but he did," Parker said. "That's just not something that you would remember."

"How would you know what I remember or don't remember?" I tried to remain calm, but the words came out quite loud, and I'm sure my frustration was showing.

"I understand that this situation can be very unsettling for you, but please, let me continue."

I said nothing, and Parker continued, "In simple terms, your father invented a way to record human memory. In other words, he could record the

11

positions of each of the tens of billions of neurons and their corresponding connections responsible for human memory. Of course, we have made progress, but we are still years away from decoding that information into something we can understand. Despite that, we thought it might be possible to imprint the recorded memory onto another human mind. It took us five years, but we finally succeeded in doing just that."

"Five years? My father just told me about his breakthrough thirty minutes ago."

"It's very complicated, Mr. Neumann. I'm afraid just over five years have passed since the last memory of your father was created," he said.

That was a weird thing to say, I thought. "What exactly does that mean?"

"You may have difficulty accepting this, Mr. Neumann, but you are not who you think you are," Parker said. "When your father put you in his machine, he recorded all your memories. We put those memories into another human being. So, your mind is that of Alex Neumann, but your body is not."

I was worried before, but now I saw this was an elaborate joke. I started laughing because I knew someone had got me good. Finally, I said, "Oh my God. This is probably the greatest practical joke I ever saw or even heard about. Who put you up to this? My wife? My dad? Am I on TV?"

"This is no joke, Mr. Neumann," Parker said. "Let me show you." With that, he unhooked the straps holding me to the bed and held out his arm to help me up, but I waved him off and sat up on the bed. I was surprised to see I was dressed in something other than a hospital garment. I had no shirt, but I was wearing black polyester pants like the security guard standing outside. The pants had a black belt, but that was it. I had no socks or shoes and no watch. I felt the front pockets. They were empty, as I expected. I didn't want to be obvious, so I didn't try to check the back pockets, but I knew they would be empty too.

Parker then seemed to realize I was underdressed and opened the door and said something to the guard. He looked around the room, presumably for a mirror, but not finding one, reached into his pocket and pulled out his phone. He tapped several buttons to bring up the camera app and handed it to me.

What I saw shocked me. The face on the screen wasn't me at all. This face was very different than mine. My dark hair and brown eyes were replaced by sandy blonde hair and blue eyes. He had a handsome face with the beginnings of a beard and looked to be in his mid-twenties, about the same age as me or the last age that I remember being. I still wasn't entirely sure it wasn't a trick, so I turned my head back and forth and raised my hand into the frame. The image followed along perfectly.

I wasn't convinced the phone was not distorting the image, so I turned it off and looked at myself in the screen's reflection. The reflection looked like the image I just saw. I then took a close look at my hands. Everyone always talks about knowing something like "the back of your hand," but the backs of my hands were different than I remembered. That is when I knew for sure it was true. My voice was also different, deeper. I first assumed an illness caused it, but that was not the case.

"I can answer any questions you might have," Parker eventually said.

"Might have?" I said as I handed the phone back to him. "I definitely have questions. First and foremost, what happened to the real me? Am I dead?"

"The real you is fine. He is living a quiet life with a wife and two kids."

"Two kids?"

"Yes, you have a four-year-old daughter and a two-year-old son. Your father told me there is another on the way, too."

The thought of having two children out there and one on the way filled me with joy and sorrow at the same time. How could I possibly be a parent to three children with a father who is not me? "Can I see them?" I said.

"I don't think that would be a good idea, but if you want, I could try to find a photograph of them," he said.

"That would be great."

"I suppose you want to know about this body you inhabit."

"That was my next question. Whoever this was, you have essentially taken his life away, and that's some sick shit if you ask me."

"This is where it gets complicated," Parker said.

"You mean it wasn't already complicated?"

He ignored my question and said, "You can never repeat what I am about to tell you. Do you understand?"

"I understand, just like the last time. No need to repeat your threats," I said as I looked at the general.

The general interjected, "Never means never, son. To this, there are no exceptions."

I just looked at him but said nothing.

Parker continued, "The government has been experimenting with cloning for several years. They harvested the DNA from some of the most physically and mentally exceptional people they could find. This person you are 'occupying' was grown from that DNA."

"Human cloning is illegal in this country and every other country as far as I know," I said.

"Do you think the government never breaks its laws?" he said.

"This body is over twenty years old," I said. "They barely had the technology to clone humans back then, and I doubt they could have kept it a secret for that long. Besides, clone or not, he was still a real person, and you took his mind from him."

"We have made great strides in cloning recently. This clone is about four months old," Parker said. "He has never been conscious and was essentially grown in a lab using accelerated growth techniques. It is quite amazing, but it is not one of this company's operations, so I can't tell you much about it. Our client provided him for us."

"You mean the Army?" I said, looking at the general.

"I'm afraid I can't tell you that," Parker said.

"Then why me? Why did you bring me back and not someone else?"

"Not long after you visited your father in his lab, we convinced him to come to work for us," he said. "With his help, we developed the means to transfer a person's mind, consciousness if you will, into a host body. Three months ago, your father corrupted the software and all the data associated with his mind-recording device, including all our recordings. He then disappeared.

"That doesn't sound like my dad. Why didn't you have backups? With something this big, I would have backups of backups."

"We did have backups," Parker said, "but the secret nature of this operation meant that we couldn't risk uploading anything to the cloud or even removing a copy from this secure facility. Your father had access to those backups, and he also corrupted that data."

"So, how did you get access to my brain scans?"

"When your father came to work for us, we bought the technology from the university. They were required to give us everything related to his invention and keep no backups, but when your father disappeared, we returned to the university hoping to find something we might have overlooked. It turns out that the data involved in copying someone's memory is so large that it requires its own hard drive. We found three removable drives that everyone overlooked, yours, one from your wife, and another from a student. We used your data to bring you back, hoping you could help us find your father."

"I find it hard to believe that a single hard drive is big enough to fit all that information," I said. "I mean, I know the human brain has a huge storage capacity. I don't know what that is, but one hard drive seems too small."

"There's actually room to spare," Parker said. "For one thing, the machine doesn't scan the entire brain, only the conscious memories. Things like muscle memory, instinct, and all the mundane tasks the brain is responsible for are not recorded. In addition, the data is compressed."

The fact that the machine did not record muscle memory surprised me and brought up some questions I decided to keep to myself for the time being. Instead, I asked, "Why didn't you just enlist the help of the real Alex Neumann?"

"We felt the odds of success were too low," Parker said. "We were certain that Alex would not leave his family for an unknown period to get involved in a search like this. Besides, we needed to test the machine on a human. If it didn't work, retrieving the lost data would have become less important."

"So, I'm just a lab rat?"

"I'm not going to sugarcoat it, Alex," Parker said. "You were a means to an end, but it worked, and you are alive and well. Now we need your help."

"If my father did what you say he did, he must have had a good reason. If I help you find him, what will you do? Put him in jail, or worse? I think you wasted your time resurrecting me, Mr. Parker." As soon as I said that, I realized how stupid I was. I needed to leave the door open, or I would be useless to them.

"We think a foreign government may have coerced your father," the general said. "There have been reports that the Russians want to acquire this technology, and they may have forced him to turn over his data and destroy it on our end. There is no evidence he took any money, so we think they threatened his life or that of a family member, perhaps your life, the other you. He might have given the Russians a copy of his research and then disappeared to avoid prosecution. Our best hope is that he gave the Russians false information and then hid to prevent retaliation. Whatever

16

the reason, he must know that his family is in danger, so he won't be able to stay hidden for long. When he is found, you would want to be sure the right people find him."

"Your story seems like quite a stretch," I said. "I also didn't hear any good reason that I should help you put my father in jail. That is where he would be going if he lives that long since your concern about the Russians being after him is probably total bullshit." I wanted him to believe I would follow his plan, but folding too soon would look suspicious. He needed to believe I was convinced.

"The thing is, Alex, your father wouldn't go to jail if you helped us find him," Parker said. "Some powerful people can't let the Russians get ahead of us on this technology. If we can find your father and get the information we need, they will give him immunity from prosecution. After all, trying to save your son is not a crime. We also wouldn't want the publicity of a trial."

He smiled after this last statement, but his smile quickly disappeared, and he said, "However, he has been put on a government watch list because finding him is extremely important to a lot of people, but if a government agency finds him first then I don't know what will happen to him."

I didn't trust him, but I did believe he would do anything to avoid publicity. The only thing I could do was play along until I could think of a way out. "Okay. I don't know how to help, but I will do what I can. I'm choosing to trust you and expect you to honor your promise."

"Of course," Parker said. "I want nothing more than to get your father back to the lab, safe and sound. You will stay here for a couple of days so the doctor can do more tests. Then we will get started."

The door opened, and the guard handed Parker a shirt. "Here," he said, "put this on," and gave me the shirt. He then turned and walked out the door. The general followed him out.

I put the shirt on. It was a white Polo shirt with the letters "PB" printed next to what looked like a strand of DNA. I assumed it was the Parker Biosystems logo. I got up and walked to the door. I thought it would be locked, but I wanted to check anyway. It was locked. I looked around the room. I wanted to see if there was another way out, but I saw none. The room had no window, not even on the door, which was heavy gauge steel. The ceiling had air vents, but they were way too small to climb through. The walls were concrete blocks, so I wasn't going through a wall. It looked like I would have to play their game a while longer.

After a few minutes, Dr. Carr returned. She put a disposable thermometer in my mouth and checked my pulse and blood pressure. She looked at the thermometer and said, "You seem in good health, Mr. Neuman. I will recommend that you be released tomorrow if nothing changes between now and then."

After she left, I sat for a long while thinking about my situation and decided that sleep was probably a good idea. I could not do much, so being well-rested before tomorrow might help me.

Just as I decided to try to sleep, there was a knock at the door, and it opened. A young woman walked in and propped the door open. She wore the outfit of a cleaning lady, like a hotel maid. Outside the door was her cart of cleaning supplies. I could see the guard was still there too. It was hard to tell from the back, but the guard looked different this time. They probably had a shift change recently, but since the room had no clock, I had no idea what time it was.

The young woman had a spray bottle in one hand and a cloth in the other. She started to wipe down the room. She looked to be Latino. I guessed she was in her late twenties, somewhat shorter than average, with her long, dark hair tied back in a ponytail. She was attractive, and I imagined she was probably stunning when she let her hair down and dressed up for a night out.

"I'm sorry for the interruption, sir," she said with a Spanish accent. "I won't be long."

I noticed her nametag said, "Gabriela." I said, "Take your time, Gabriela. I can use the company."

She looked down at her nametag and back at me, saying, "Most people call me Gabby."

"It's very nice to meet you, Gabby."

"It is nice to meet you too, sir."

"Alex. My name is Alex."

"Alex," she repeated. "It is nice to meet you, Alex."

She wiped down the equipment near me and quietly said, "Don't look up. This room is monitored. I'm a friend of your father's. If you want to leave here, be ready in one hour. When I leave, turn out the lights and pretend to sleep."

"I have no shoes," I said.

"Don't worry. One hour," she said. She then continued to clean in silence for a few minutes. I kept quiet, too, not knowing if there were microphones as well as cameras in the room. As Gabby left the room, she looked me in the eyes but said nothing.

I did what she said. After she left, I flipped the switch at the door, lay on the bed, and waited. Most of the small amount of light in the room was coming from under the door. I tried to locate the camera, but it was too dark. I figured it was also too dark for the camera to see me unless it had night vision. Either way, whoever monitored the cameras would get bored watching after a while, which was probably her intention.

I waited in the dark for what seemed like well over an hour, and then I heard three light taps on the door. I jumped out of bed and headed toward the door. It opened slightly, and the woman, Gabby, stuck her head in and said, "Come on!"

I slipped out the door as quickly as possible and looked around. The guard at the door was gone. "Where is the guard?"

"The guard is not needed this late. Here, put these on. They belong to my brother. I hope they fit."

She handed me a pair of used tennis shoes. They were in good shape, but I was apprehensive about putting my bare feet into someone else's shoes. I decided it was the least of my worries at the time and quickly slipped them on. They were slightly big, but I knew that was way better than slightly small. I tied them up and followed Gabby down the nearest hallway, where she had her cleaning cart. She lifted the towel hanging from the side, revealing a small, empty cavity. "Get in," she said.

I wasn't sure if I could fit, but I sat down inside the cart, bent my head, pulled my knees up, and squeezed inside. She put the towel back in place and pushed me and the cart for another twenty or thirty feet. She then turned to the right, and we got on an elevator. I expected Gabby to say something at this point but heard only silence. I assumed the elevator was also being monitored, so I remained quiet. Once we were off the elevator, I heard a male voice say, "Hi, Gabby. I see you are working late tonight."

"Yes. There were extra rooms that needed cleaning tonight."

"Well, you have a good night. See you next week."

"You too, Joe. See you next week."

Chapter 4

Another minute ticked by before we stopped, and Gabby pushed aside the towel and said, "You can get out now."

I got out next to a large, white van with the words "Ramirez Commercial Cleaning Services" on the side. I felt a chill in the air. A man came around from the back of the van wearing a uniform like Gabby's. He was also Latino, about average height, and maybe 30 years old. He was clean-shaven and had dark, medium-length hair parted on the side. "This is my brother, David," Gabby said.

I reached out my hand, but he ignored it, grabbed the cart, pulled it toward the back of the van where the doors were open, and said, "We need to go."

Gabby opened the side door, pulled out a jacket, and handed it to me. It was a black leather motorcycle jacket. Very nice. I put it on, and she said, "Get in! Quickly!"

I climbed inside and closed the door while Gabby got into the passenger seat and David got into the driver's seat. The van had no back seats and was full of cleaning equipment, so I found a space and sat on the floor. As David put the van in drive, Gabby reached behind the seat, grabbed what looked like a tarp, and handed it to me. "Cover yourself," she said.

I could see the exit we were coming up on had a gate and a guard house, so I put the tarp over me and lay on the floor. We stopped at the gate, and after a brief conversation with the guard, I could see the inside of the van illuminated by a flashlight. I held my breath, and we drove past the gate a few seconds later. I removed the tarp and sat up. "What now?" I asked.

"That's a good question," David said while looking at Gabby sternly. "I agreed to help you only because I knew you would be foolish enough to try this alone, but have you thought about the consequences of your actions? We certainly can't go back to work there, and who knows what kind of trouble we will be in with the police."

"Relax, David," she said. "We didn't break any laws. If anyone committed a crime, it was Parker. Unless the laws have changed in America, a corporation can't hold people prisoner. Besides, there are many more credible suspects than us."

"That may be true," he said, "but Parker is a powerful man with powerful contacts in the government. You should cut this guy loose, or you will be in the same danger as him."

"Just stick to the plan, and everything will be fine," Gabby said. "Once you drop us off, go home and act like nothing has changed. If anyone asks, tell them I had to leave to care for poor, sick Mama."

"Wonderful plan, Sis. I hope nobody realizes our mother died sixteen years ago."

A few minutes later, we entered the parking lot of a modern-looking Hilton hotel. I assumed if we were going to hide out, it would be in some seedy hotel. This wasn't the Ritz-Carlton, but it was better than I expected.

David stopped by the front doors, and Gabby and I got out. She pulled out a small suitcase from the back of the van. It was a black, soft-sided piece with wheels and a handle that pulled out. I reached out my hand and offered to take it for her. She smiled and handed it to me. I followed her inside while David drove away.

We walked up to the front desk, and a young man with pasty white skin and slicked-back dark hair greeted us. I smiled, thinking he might be the son of Dracula. "Good evening, folks," he said. "Can I help you?"

"Yes," Gabby said. "We have a reservation for John and Maria Miller."

He tapped at his computer and said, "Yes, I have you here. I need your ID and a credit card for the room, please."

Gabby handed him her license and credit card, and he said he would be right back and went into the back office, presumably to make a copy of the license. I looked at Gabby and whispered, "Miller?"

"My brother has many connections," she said quietly. You don't think I only needed him to drive, do you?"

The man came back and handed Gabby her license. "The total for tonight is 135 plus a 200-dollar deposit that will come off after your stay."

"Fine," Gabby said and handed him a credit card.

The man ran her credit card and handed it back to her along with some paperwork and two key cards. "You are in 209. Take the elevator to the second floor and then turn right."

We thanked the man and then headed up to the room. It was nice but basic. It had two queen beds and a large television but no refrigerator. I supposed we wouldn't be there long, so we didn't need it. Gabby put the suitcase on the bed and started to unzip it when I said, "We need to talk."

She stopped what she was doing and turned to look at me. She sat on the edge of the bed and said, "I know you must have many questions. Ask me anything."

"Why are you helping me?"

"Your father was my friend. You may see me as a dumb immigrant that can't do anything but clean office buildings for a living, but I am so much more than that. I have a successful company, and I'm taking classes online to earn a business degree."

I interrupted her and said, "Hold on! To be clear, the thought of you being a dumb immigrant never crossed my mind."

"I'm sorry," she said, "I guess I get a little defensive because so many people seem to look down on me if they notice me at all. Anyway, my point is, I was interested in your father's work, and he was happy to talk to me about it. I learned a lot about not only what he was doing but also what others in the company were doing."

"Others? You mean Scott Parker?"

"Your father wanted to use his research to help people, but when he found out what Parker had planned for the technology, well . . ." She paused momentarily and said, "I think he just couldn't let it happen."

"From what I understand, the goal is to duplicate the minds of highly skilled military personnel, like special forces. I imagine it takes many years of extensive and expensive training to produce a Navy Seal or Green Beret. Now we can produce dozens of them in a few months. I get why Dad would be unhappy about that, and I understand the ethical issues, but I don't know why he would sacrifice his freedom and possibly his life for this. I mean, this seems relatively minor compared to some of the things the government has done in the past."

"I don't know everything. Perhaps he discovered something even worse. Or maybe his values are just different than yours."

I felt slightly insulted by that, but I don't think she intended it that way. Perhaps I was less caring than I should have been. I thought that the good outweighed the bad, but I didn't know the extent of the bad. I said, "One thing I don't understand, well, one of many things, is how you knew who I was. I mean, I don't even know who I am right now."

"I didn't know, not a hundred percent. I learned from your dad what his machine could do. When I saw your name on the chart outside the door, I just put two and two together. I figured if I was wrong, you would let me know."

"Do you know where my father is, Gabby?"

"No, I have no idea. His decision to do what he did must have been sudden because he didn't mention anything to me when I last saw him. Do you have any idea?"

"No, not really. I don't even know where we are."

"We are in a hotel just outside of **Fredericksburg, Virginia**," she said as she opened her suitcase and handed me some clothes. "These are for tomorrow. They are my brother's but should fit you.

24

"Do you know where my father lives?" I asked.

"He rents a house not too far from here. I'm sure he wouldn't be foolish enough to go there."

"What about his house in Florida?"

"He told me he is renting it out. He wouldn't be able to go there anyway. I'm sure both of those houses have been checked out."

Gabby picked up her purse and phone and said, "I need to go out for about an hour. We need supplies."

"I'll come with you," I said. I had no desire to be cooped up in a hotel room alone.

"I don't think that would be a good idea. They probably don't know you are missing yet, but when they do, you can be sure they will check security cameras. It's best to keep you away from cameras as much as possible."

"I'm certain the hotel has me on camera," I said.

"Yes, but I'm sure private cameras are not easily accessible like public cameras are."

I couldn't argue with that, but I asked, "How will you get there?"

"There's a small shopping plaza down the road. It's not too far to walk."

After she left, I sat on the bed and took off the shoes that Gabby had given me. My feet felt sweaty without socks on. I looked in the bag and found a pair of socks and put them on. I turned on the news but then had a better idea. I put the shoes back on, put my key card in my pocket, and went to the lobby.

At the reception desk, I asked if they had computers for guests to use. He pointed me to a nearby room with three computers on a long table against the left wall. Each computer was separated by a divider that gave the user a little privacy. Since the room was empty, I didn't need it.

I wanted to learn about myself or my former self. Hell, I didn't know how to think about my other self. Part of me thought of him as the real me, but deep down, I knew there could only be one me, and he wasn't me. Even so, I wanted to find out more about my wife and kids, which is to say, Alex's wife and kids. It was difficult to know that the woman I loved and the children that should have been mine belonged to another man who was me and not me.

I typed my name into Google, which returned sixteen million results. Surprisingly, there are a lot of people with my name. I looked through the first few pages and decided to go to Facebook. I tried to log in, but Alex changed the password. I wasn't too surprised. Every six months or so, there seems to be a significant data breach that causes everyone to change their passwords.

Since I was not logged in, I couldn't do much on Facebook. I remembered the address of my profile page and typed it in. It showed some basic information about me but nothing else. I saw a small profile photo that looked like a professional photographer had taken it. Lisa and I were sitting, each holding a child. I was holding a beautiful, smiling little girl, about two or three years old, while Lisa was holding a baby, perhaps a few months old. I guessed the photo was at least a year old. Seeing it made me both happy and sad. I remember thinking that I should have asked Parker their names, but I didn't, which made me feel like a terrible father.

I closed the browser and got up to head back to my room. While waiting for the elevator, two hotel employees walked toward me. One was about thirty with short, blonde hair. He was giving instructions to a young man that was eighteen at best. They both looked at me as they approached, and the older man said, "Good evening, Sir." He looked away and quickly looked back at me excitedly, "John?" he said. "Oh, my God! Annie said you disappeared. What happened to you? Where have you been?"

I didn't know what to say at that moment. Was this an innocent mistake, or was my body a clone of someone this guy knew? I needed to find out more but couldn't think of what to say, so I said, "I'm afraid you have me confused with someone else."

"I think I would recognize my sister's fiancée," the man said.

I looked at his nametag, which read, "Michael Hansen, Assistant Manager." "Mr. Hansen," I said, "who exactly do you think I am?"

"So that's how we're playing this?" he said. "Okay, I think you are exactly Jonathan Thomas. You are, or were, engaged to be married to my sister, Annette Hansen. Or did you forget?"

I looked at him for a moment, not knowing what to say.

"I get it, John," he said. "You got cold feet, but running away is a coward's way out. It's certainly not what I expected from a former Army Ranger." He shook his head in disgust and walked away.

I didn't like that I might have ruined the memory of a man who probably deserved much better. I felt like I should go after him and explain the situation, but what would I say that wouldn't make me look like I was not only a liar but a crazy one at that?

I got back to the room about five minutes before Gabby arrived with a couple of bags in her hands. One bag had four bottles of water, a box of granola bars, and some bananas. It was not exactly what I expected. I'm not sure why, but when she said she was going out for supplies, I half expected her to return with ingredients to make pipe bombs.

She took a small smartphone from the other bag and said, "I got you a phone. It's anonymous so that no one can track you. This way, we can keep in touch if we get separated."

I started feeling a little guilty about everything she had been doing for me and said, "Listen, I very much appreciate what you have done for me, but things could get dangerous, and I wouldn't want something bad to happen to you because of me. Go home. Nobody knows you helped me. Just play dumb. If they question you, tell them the security guard had been acting unusual."

"Let's talk about this tomorrow," she said. "I think we should get some sleep now. You can have this bed, and I'll take the one by the window."

She moved over to the other bed and removed her shirt and pants. She was wearing a sexy white bra and panties that revealed a very fit and almost perfectly shaped form. She caught me looking at her and said, "Don't get any ideas. I have a boyfriend that you don't want to mess with." She then got into bed and turned out her light.

"Don't worry. I'm happily married. At least I was yesterday," I said, not knowing what to think about my current situation.

I removed my clothes except for my underwear and got into bed too. I usually sleep naked, but it didn't seem appropriate under the circumstances. I turned off my light and said, "Where is your boyfriend now?"

"Go to sleep," she said.

Chapter 5

I woke up to a tap on my shoulder. I opened my eyes and saw Gabby standing over me with a towel wrapped around her body. She was brushing her hair and said, "You should get up now. The shower is free."

I looked at the window, and even though the curtains were drawn, I could see the sun had not come up yet. I then looked at the clock on my nightstand. It read 5:53. "Are you an owl?" I asked. "Have you seen the time?"

"Do you think sleeping all day is a good idea?"

"Not all day, but some of the day would be nice," I said as I got out of bed.

I went into the bathroom and noticed myself in the mirror as I got undressed to take a shower. I saw myself in the mirror before but never looked closely. I was muscular without an ounce of excess fat. As much as I didn't like being in someone else's body, this was something I could get used to. I thought about how I disliked vain people, but after seeing myself, I couldn't help feeling a bit of pride and even smugness about how I looked. I tried to shrug off that feeling as I got into the shower.

The hotel had a complimentary breakfast, and we were there when it opened at 7:00 a.m. There wasn't a large selection, but it was enough for me. I put some bacon and eggs on my plate, a waffle, and two pieces of toast. Gabby was ahead of me in line and picked out a table near a window. I sat down across from her. The breakfast room was on the first floor at the front of the hotel. Through the window, I saw a young couple heading to their car, pulling large suitcases behind them. I also saw a man in a suit carrying a briefcase in one hand and a small suitcase in the other. It was quite busy at 7 a.m.

I looked at Gabby and said, "I like your company and appreciate you breaking me out of that place, but it would be best if we parted ways here.

You have done way more than any decent person would do in a situation like this."

"I'm not leaving you," she said casually as she took a bite of her bagel.

"Why is it so important for you to help me?"

She finished chewing her bagel and swallowed. "I care about your father almost as much as you do. I very much want to find him and make sure he is okay. I am willing to take the risk."

I took the phone she gave me out of my pocket and held it up. "I'll call you if I find him."

"I'll tell you what," she said. "I have people who can handle my business for a while. How about I give you a week? If we can't find Bernie by then, I will go home."

I got the feeling that this girl would not give up, so I said, "Fine. I suppose I can put up with you for a week."

She smiled and said, "You're a funny guy. Keep it up, and you'll be stuck with me for two weeks."

"Well, I could probably think of a few worse fates."

"If you want to get rid of me, we should probably think about how we will find your dad. Do you have any idea where he might be?"

"I thought we could start at the house he rents here and then head down to Florida if we don't find anything there."

"Okay," Gabby said. "I doubt we will find anything useful there, but you never know."

Gabby called a local car rental office from our room, and they sent someone to the hotel to pick us up. Once there, Gabby used her fake id and credit card to rent a car. I wondered if she would pay the credit card bill or if it was a stolen number. I decided it was best not to ask.

The counter agent reviewed the available cars and said he had two Mustang convertibles and could give us one for the same price as a mid-size sedan. Gabby jumped on the idea of a convertible and said, "We'll take the Mustang."

"You do realize that it's too cold to put the top down, which is why they lowered the price?" I said.

"You do realize that we will probably drive it to Florida?"

"Touché," I said. I couldn't argue that logic.

Once the paperwork was done, I put our stuff in the trunk and started to get into the driver's seat when Gabby grabbed my arm and said, "What do you think you're doing?"

"I thought I would drive first," I said. "Do you have a problem with that?"

"Tell me, what will you do if the police pull you over?"

I didn't think about that. I had nothing, no license, no credit card, and no cash. I walked around and got into the passenger seat while Gabby sat in the driver's seat. "After careful consideration," I said, "I think it would be best if you drive."

She looked at me briefly, smiled, and shook her head before starting the engine.

We drove for ten or fifteen minutes and ended up in an older part of town. We stopped at a two-story home that looked similar to most other homes on the street. It had a large, covered porch. Five pillars were holding up the roof to the porch. Stairs were going up on the left and the right with a small gap between them. The house had no driveway, so we parallel-parked on the street in front of it.

Gabby and I got out of the car and walked toward the house. There were two front doors. The left was labeled "A," and the right was labeled "B." The right door had caution tape over it.

"This looks like a duplex," I said.

"It is," Gabby said.

"I thought you said he was renting a house."

"This is a house. What are you talking about?"

"Never mind," I said. I didn't picture Dad living in a duplex, but it made sense since he lived alone.

We approached the door with caution tape. I looked around and saw no one looking, so I pulled the tape off one side and noticed the door was broken. It looked like someone kicked it open or hit it with something heavy. I pushed it open, and we went inside.

It looked very quaint. It had old wood floors that were polished to a nice shine. The living room was simple. A sofa and chair were on one side, and a television on a TV stand on the other. Only one picture hung on the wall. It was a picture of Mom and Dad with me when I graduated high school.

The small kitchen had an old gas stove and an even older refrigerator. When I opened the refrigerator, I saw only a few condiments on the door. Everything else was cleaned out. The cabinets were mostly filled with dishes, but the pantry was empty.

"He probably gave most of his food away to a neighbor or someone before he left," I said.

We went upstairs, where we found two bedrooms. One had a double-size bed and one dresser. That was it. Nothing hung on the walls. I checked the closet. Several dress shirts and pants were hanging there, but I saw no casual clothes. I also saw a heavy coat but no light jacket.

"Looks like he took his casual clothes and left the dressy stuff behind," I said. "He also left his heavy coat behind."

"He must have headed to Florida," Gabby said.

"I agree."

We checked the second bedroom. Inside was a desk but no computer or laptop. There was also a bookcase with several books related to neurology, memory, and even computer programming, but we found nothing that would give away Dad's destination.

We left there and got back on the road, heading for Florida. The first couple of hours went smoothly. Gabby told me about moving to the United States from Mexico when she was twelve years old. She said her father was a police chief who worked hard to bring down a local drug cartel. Unfortunately, many police officers were corrupt, and his efforts were met with much resistance. One day, her mother was found dead, the victim of a drug overdose. It was ruled a suicide, but Gabby's father knew it was a warning. To protect his children, he sought asylum in the United States. In exchange, he told them everything he knew about the cartel and all the cops he suspected were working for them.

I could tell she was uncomfortable talking about it, so I spoke a little about my life, but she seemed to know a lot about me already. I assumed her talks with Dad were about more than just science.

When we crossed the border into North Carolina, Gabby wanted to stop for gas and use the washroom, so we got off the highway and stopped at a gas station. I told her I would be happy to pump the gas, so she swiped her card at the pump and headed to the washroom. When I finished pumping the gas, I figured I should go, too, since I had no idea when we would stop again.

I didn't see Gabby when I came out of the washroom and figured she was waiting for me in the car, but she was not. It was another five minutes before she returned, and I decided not to ask her what had taken so long. It was probably a female thing that I did not want to know about. I was just happy that she picked up a few snacks on her way out.

We pushed on until we were close to Jacksonville and then stopped for dinner. We went to an Italian Restaurant because, despite her Mexican heritage, she loved Italian food. I shouldn't have been surprised because I love Italian food too and don't have an ounce of Italian in me. Well, at least the other me doesn't.

After dinner, we hit the road again. I think we both wanted to get there as soon as possible. We were tired and wanted to rest. By the time we reached my hometown, it was almost ten o'clock. I wanted to drive by Alex's house, and although it was late, Gabby had no problem doing that.

We stopped one house away and turned off the lights. I didn't recognize the two cars in the driveway, but I wasn't surprised. Five years had passed, and I didn't expect everything to stay the same. The curtains were drawn, but we could see a light in the living room. The rest of the house was dark. The kids were probably in bed, and Lisa and the other me were most likely watching television.

"Let's go," I said. "I know a hotel nearby."

Gabby looked at me thoughtfully but said nothing. She just put the car in drive and drove away.

The hotel wasn't far. It was a nice little place with a view of the intercostal waterway. We again got a room with two queen beds. The room was facing west with a great view of the water. Even though it was dark, I could see several sailboats anchored in the waterway and the lights from Clearwater Beach in the distance.

"I never get tired of this view," I said.

"Yes, it's nice," Gabby said absently as she sat on the bed, looking at her phone.

"Did you even see it?" I said as I turned to look at her.

"Yes, I saw it when we got here, but I am busy with something right now."

"What are you doing?"

"I still have a business to run even though I am not there. I'm answering emails from customers and prospects, sending out invoices, and ordering supplies. You know, business stuff."

"Of course," I said. "This trip must make your job a lot harder. I feel bad that I got you into this."

"None of this is your fault. Besides, my life was getting to be way too routine. It feels good to be doing something meaningful."

I turned and looked back out the window. It felt like we were on a mission, but I couldn't help but wonder how meaningful it was. If Dad was still alive and we did manage to find him, then what? Would he know who I am? Would he turn himself in? Could I even trust Parker to keep his word? Working with computers was comforting because there was always a level of certainty. Now I felt lost and unsure of myself. "I'm going out for a walk," I told Gabby, quickly leaving before she could object.

There is a trail along the waterfront that the town calls a "linear park." I got on it and started walking. I suddenly felt an urge to run, which was an urge I hadn't felt since childhood, so I ran. I ran steadily for almost a mile and then slowed to a walk when I reached the marina near the heart of town. I was surprised that I was only slightly winded. I felt like I could have turned around and run back with no problem. The old me couldn't run to the end of the block without getting tired. I decided I liked this feeling, and I was going to try to keep in shape.

When I returned to the hotel, Gabby was sitting on the bed watching the news. She didn't look at me when I came in, but after several long seconds, she put the television on mute, turned to me, and said, "Feeling better?"

"Better?" I asked. "Better than what?"

"Something is obviously on your mind. I figured you went out for a walk to clear your head."

"I'm fine. I just have many questions floating around in my mind with no clear answers."

"Did that walk help clear any of them up?" she asked.

"I'm afraid not," I said. It added to my long list of questions, but I didn't feel like mentioning that to her.

"Well, it's late. Maybe a good night's sleep will help clear your head."

With that, she proceeded to undress for bed. I'm not sure why she felt so comfortable stripping down to her underwear in front of me while at the same time keeping me at a distance because of her boyfriend. Perhaps she just got off on teasing men. I wondered if her boyfriend knew she behaved like this. I let the thought cross my mind for a moment that I was special, but I knew better.

We were up early the following day and headed to the lobby, where a breakfast buffet was set up. I got coffee and some bacon and eggs and sat with Gabby, who had granola, a yogurt, and a glass of orange juice. I said, "I'm still thinking about what I'm going to say when we get there."

"Worrying won't help," Gabby said. "Just go with the flow. You will think of it when the time comes."

"I hope so. I've never met myself before, and seeing my wife with another man might freak me out a little, even if that man is me."

"Maybe I should go without you."

"No, I can handle it, but you can come with me to help if I get stuck."

"I wouldn't miss it for the world."

"I'm not sure how I should take that."

"Take it any way you want. You need to understand that you are not Alex anymore, and Lisa is not your wife," she said. "Remember, the memories in your head were implanted. They are someone else's memories. You are not that person. From here on, the life you live is your own."

I nodded in reluctant agreement, and then she said, "Hey, you need your own identity," and excitedly dug through her purse and came out with a driver's license. "I just remembered my brother got this for you."

She handed me the card, and I noticed it said "John Miller" and was a very good copy of a Virginia driver's license. At least, I assumed it was a good copy, having never seen one before. It did not exactly look like me, although it was similar. "Where did you get the photo?" I asked.

"I told David what you looked like, and he found a photo that matched the description," she said. "We were in a hurry. Don't worry. Nobody checks photos carefully. I just wouldn't show it to a cop. If anyone can look it up, they will find it's fake."

I put the ID in my pocket, and we finished breakfast without saying much more.

We checked out and then got in the car for the longest five-minute ride of my life. When we arrived, Gabby parked on the street in front of the house and said, "Are you ready?"

"As ready as I'll ever be," I said, and we both got out of the car and walked to the front door.

Chapter 6

Gabby rang the bell, and I heard children screaming inside the house while we waited. Not bad screaming but more like squeals of delight from young kids playing. At that moment, I wished I could trade places with the real Alex. Then I realized I was probably the first person in the world to be envious of himself.

Lisa answered the door. She was dressed in yoga pants and an oversized t-shirt that did nothing to hide the obvious baby bump. I was overwhelmed by the thought that I learned I would be a father just the other day, and now a third child was on the way. I was speechless.

Abbey must have sensed my anxiety and stepped forward and said, "Hi, we are friends of Alex's father. Is he here?"

"We've already talked to the police," Lisa said. "Why don't you speak to them?"

By now, I had regained my ability to speak and said, "His father is in great danger, and we think we can help. We are both very fond of him, and we don't want any harm to come to him."

Lisa looked at me very carefully as if trying to decide if I was seriously concerned or if I was someone meaning to do him harm. I guessed she saw something she liked in me and said, "Just a minute," before shutting the door.

The door opened again after what felt like an hour but was probably thirty seconds. This time I was looking at myself, which seemed stranger than seeing Lisa as someone she didn't know. The real me was sporting a beard and mustache, which I always found too itchy to last more than a few weeks. Lisa must have talked him into it. I remember Lisa being disappointed the last time I shaved my fledgling beard.

"I've already told the police everything I know about my father," Alex said.

38

"We are not police officers and don't know what you told them. My name is John, and this is Gabby. We are friends of your father's. Some people have painted him a traitor to his country. If the authorities find him, I don't think you will hear about it on the news, if you know what I mean. I believe he had a good reason for doing what he did. I think maybe he learned something he wasn't supposed to know."

Alex interrupted me and said, "Are you saying he is some kind of whistleblower? Don't you have to, I don't know, blow a whistle?"

"Maybe he's too scared," Gabby offered. "Maybe he is sitting on information that powerful people don't want to be released and is afraid his family might be in danger if he does release it. You might be in danger."

"Look," Alex said, "this all seems a bit far-fetched. If my father thought I was in danger, he would have found a way to contact me, but he hasn't. Even if he had contacted me, I probably wouldn't tell you. For all I know, you two are the ones after him."

I hesitated momentarily and then said, "Do you remember when you were fifteen and got your learner's permit? Your dad taught you how to drive his Jeep with a standard transmission. You wanted him to teach you in your mom's Oldsmobile, which was an automatic, but he refused. He said life wouldn't always be easy, and you needed to get used to overcoming challenges."

"He was right about life not being easy," Alex said. "How did you know about that?"

"We worked together for years," I said. "Bernie told me lots of stories. We spent many hours in the lab together. Your father talked a lot about you. He cares a lot about you."

"He had a funny way of showing it."

"He's a good man. He's not perfect, but I would be lucky to have a father like yours." I surprised myself when I said that because I meant it.

39

I believe you want to help my father, but I truly have not heard from him since he disappeared. I wish he would have told me he was okay, but he didn't. If you find him, please let me know how he is and where he is."

"We will," I said. "We truly do want to help your dad."

I took out my phone and was about to text Alex, but I thought it would be suspicious if I knew his number, so I said, "What is your phone number?"

He told me his number, and I typed a text saying, "This is John. If you think of anything else, please let me know."

Once we were back in the car, Gabby asked me, "Do you believe him?"

"I think he is telling the truth," I said. "I was never a good liar. Unless he has changed over the last five years, I assume my father never contacted him. The question then is why? Why did my father never contact his only son?"

"Maybe he wanted to keep him safe like you said."

"Exactly. He knew people would be monitoring his family and friends, so to keep them safe and reduce the chance of being found, he would need help from someone far less obvious."

"Like whom?" Gabby said.

"Whom?" I said, laughing. "Sounds like someone has been studying English grammar."

"Okay, okay," Gabby said while trying to hold back a laugh. "Like who? Do I sound more American now?"

"Just like a native."

We sat in silence for about thirty seconds, and then Gabby finally said, "Well, are you going to tell me who you are thinking about?"

"Are you up for a drive to Tampa?" I asked.

Chapter 7

We drove for a little over a half hour. During the drive, we discussed what we would do if we found Dad. We never came up with a solution to the problem because there was a big unknown. That unknown was what Dad learned that caused him to do what he did.

The GPS on Gabby's phone led us to the driveway of an old, two-story brick home with a nicely landscaped lawn and a beautiful view of Tampa Bay. "Okay, we're here," Gabby said. "So now, are you going to tell me whose house this is, or do you like keeping me in suspense?"

I did like keeping her in suspense, although I'm not sure why. Maybe I felt like she controlled almost everything we did on this trip, and I wanted to take back some of that power. "This is the home of Dr. William Patterson, a former colleague and a friend of my father," I said.

"Do you think your father contacted him?"

"I think he might have, but I don't know for sure."

"I would think Parker and his people have already checked out all of your father's friends," Gabby said.

"I'm sure that is probably true," I said, "but Bill Patterson is the only one of Dad's friends that I can think of that has the intelligence, the means, and the willingness to help him disappear. Of course, he probably made several friends while in Virginia, like yourself, but I don't know them. Besides, we are here in Florida now, so let's see what he has to say."

I knocked on the front door, and a young woman answered. She wore a white polo shirt with an embroidered logo saying, "Sweet Home Tampa Senior Care." That was surprising, and I wondered if Dr. Bill was sick.

"Can I help you?" the woman said.

"Hi," I said. "We're looking for Dr. Bill. I mean Dr. Patterson. Is he available?"

"I'm so sorry to tell you this, but William Patterson died about three months ago," she said.

I was a bit surprised and saddened to hear that. I didn't know him all that well, but I did like him. "I'm sorry to hear that," I said. "What about Mrs. Patterson? Is she here?"

"Can I ask what your relationship is with Mrs. Patterson?" she asked, like it was her job to protect her.

"My father was friends with her husband," I said, forgetting who I was supposed to be.

She looked at me and Gabby and said, "I assume it has been a while since you last saw Mrs. Patterson," she said.

"It's been well over five years," I said, wondering what she was getting at.

"Mrs. Patterson suffers from a moderate degree of dementia," she said. "Her daughter is taking care of her, and I come while the daughter is at work. She may not even know who you are, although some days are better than others."

"We are trying to find my father, who is missing," I said. "We were hoping she might have some information for us."

"Maybe you can help," Gabby interrupted. "Has a middle-aged white man visited her recently that you know of?"

"I'm sorry," the woman said, "I have not seen anyone like that, but I only work five days a week."

"I'd like to talk to Mrs. Patterson," I said. "It's probably a long shot, but she may be of some help."

"Very well. Come on in," she said as she stepped aside to let us pass.

Once inside, we could see Mrs. Patterson on a Lazy-boy type chair watching a game show. I think it was Jeopardy, but I am not too familiar with all the game shows on television.

"Patricia," the woman called out, "you have visitors."

Patricia Patterson picked up the remote control, hit the mute button, and turned to look at us as we walked into the living room. "Hello," she said. "Can I help you?"

"Hello, Mrs. Patterson," I said. "You may not remember me, but I'm Alex Neumann. Bernie is my father." Considering her condition, I used my real name, thinking she wouldn't remember me.

"Alex? Yes, of course. I remember you," she said. "My, you have grown. It seems like just yesterday you were a teenager."

"It is good to see you again, Mrs. Patterson," I said, thinking she seemed perfectly fine.

"Please, sit down," she said, motioning us to the sofa.

Gabby took a seat on the far end of the sofa. A large ginger cat was sleeping on the other end, so I sat in the middle next to Gabby.

Mrs. Patterson looked at Gabby and said, "Who is this lovely lady you are with?"

"I'm his girlfriend," Gabby said, shooting me a look that said I should keep my mouth shut. "My name is Gabby."

"We are looking for my dad," I said, trying to cut the pleasantries short. "He is missing, and we would like to know if you have seen him."

"He went to Bill's Heaven," she said.

Gabby and I looked at each other, confused. "What do you mean?" I said.

"He's on Heaven," she said.

"You mean he's in Heaven?" I said.

Now she looked confused, "Yes, I guess you could say it that way. When you go there, can you tell Bill to hurry home? He missed dinner yesterday, and I would hate for him to miss it again. We're having lasagna."

I guess I was wrong, I thought. Obviously, we were not going to get any useful information from Mrs. Patterson, so I stood up and said, "It was lovely seeing you again, Mrs. Patterson. We will be sure to tell Dr. Bill about the lasagna."

As we were leaving, I left my phone number with the home health worker and asked her to ask the daughter if she might have seen my father. I didn't think it would amount to anything, but it was worth a shot.

Once we got back in the car, I said, "That is sad to see. It reminds me of what my mother went through."

"That must have been tough on you," Gabby said.

"It always seems sad when it happens to other people. When it happens to your own family, it's tragic."

"I'm so sorry."

"Let's talk about something else."

"Okay," she said. "Do you have any other ideas?"

"No, but I can't help feeling that what she said about Heaven was somewhat familiar, but I can't quite put my finger on it."

I'm sure if you've ever been to church, that word would be familiar to you."

"Maybe, but it seems familiar in another way. I wish I could tell you why, but I don't know."

I was distracted by the reference to Heaven for the entire ride back to the hotel. When we got to our room, I asked Gabby for her laptop. She asked me what I was looking for, but all I could say was, "I don't know yet. I'll know it when I see it."

I opened her computer and searched for "Heaven." All of the results on the first couple of pages had to do with the divine. I then tried Facebook. Unfortunately, I couldn't do much without being logged in. "I need to get into Facebook," I said to Gabby. "What's your login information?"

"I'm sorry, Alex," Gabby said, "but I'm not on Facebook."

"You're not on Facebook? Who the hell is not on Facebook?"

"Plenty of people are not on Facebook," she said defensively. "Some of us don't like having corporate giants tracking our every move."

She had a valid point. I hadn't considered the privacy issue, but I was sure that a lot had changed since I last used the service. "I didn't mean to criticize," I said. "I like that you are more of a lone wolf than a sheep in a herd."

"Thanks," she said with a slight hint of a blush. "Don't you have a Facebook account that you can use? I mean the other you."

"The other me changed his password," I said.

A big smile appeared on Gabby's face as she said, "I bet I know someone who could guess the new password."

She was right. If anyone could guess the password, it was me. I clicked the login button, entered my email address, and stopped to think. When I had to change a password previously, I used the same one with a slight variance. I grabbed a piece of paper and pen and wrote down the password

I remembered. I then wrote down several variations of it, changing just the number or symbol.

I typed the first password. The box turned red, and I got an error that read, "The password you've entered is incorrect."

"How many wrong guesses do you get before they cut you off?" I asked.

After a couple of seconds of silence, I looked up to see Gabby on the phone. She put the phone over her chest and said, "I'm ordering dinner. What would you like?"

"I am not picky," I said. "Whatever you want is fine with me, just nothing spicy, please."

I realized it was stupid to ask someone with no Facebook account how many wrong passwords they give you, so I decided to try until I couldn't try anymore. I put in the second password with no luck. I then tried the third and fourth passwords, but they were wrong too. I was surprised I was given a fifth try, but I was pretty sure it was do-or-die time. I put in the fifth password, and to my shock, I was in.

I went to the search bar and typed "William Patterson." The name was way more common than I imagined, so I added "Tampa" to the inquiry. That gave me about a dozen names, and I quickly found the right one and clicked on it.

Once on his page, I clicked on the "photos" tab. A grid of photos came up, with the latest being on top. The first photo was of Dr. Bill and his wife sitting in chairs at the beach. I scrolled down, not knowing what I was looking for. He had many photos of his wife and some of their grown kids. There were even a few of my father in the mix. I continued scrolling until one image jumped out at me.

I clicked on the photo to make it bigger. It was a picture of my father sitting on the back of Dr. Bill's boat. They would occasionally go fishing together on the weekend. Dad was smiling in the photo. He had a beer in one hand, and his pole was propped up next to him.

I looked up at Gabby and said, "I think I found something."

She came over next to me, peered over my shoulder at the screen, and said, "What did you find?"

"It's the boat," I said. "I don't know the exact name of the boat, but I'm almost positive it has the word 'Heaven' in it. That is why the word seemed so familiar to me."

"I think you're on to something. Where is the boat now?"

"I don't know."

"You don't know?" she said, a bit annoyed. "How can you not know? You know the boat's name, so you've seen it."

"I went out with them on it once as a kid," I said. "I was probably ten or twelve, and I didn't pay attention to where we were going. Besides, there is no way to know if it's still in the same marina."

"I don't think many people would switch marinas unless they move," Gabby said. "Did he move since you were a kid?"

"No. I'm pretty sure he was living in the same house."

"We should probably find the closest marina to his home and work out from there."

"No. We were in the Gulf after only ten or fifteen minutes, so I think it is somewhere along the coast here. My memory is sketchy at best, but I would guess it is between fifteen and thirty minutes from this area."

"Can you bring up a map of the area?" she said.

I typed "marinas in Pinellas County, Florida" in the search bar and hit enter. A small map popped up, and I clicked on it to expand it. It was a map of the county with a dozen or so marinas. I scrolled in on one of them, and more marinas appeared. I scrolled in even further, and even more marinas showed up.

"Holy crap!" I said. "There are more marinas than car dealers around here. This will be like finding a needle in a haystack."

After a few minutes of looking, we heard a knock at the door. Gabby grabbed some cash out of her purse and opened the door. She handed over the money, and the delivery guy pulled a pizza out of his bag and handed it to Gabby. She brought it inside and said, "Forget about the marina for now. Let's eat."

I was happy to take a break. I had not realized how hungry I was until I opened the box and laid my eyes on that cheesy goodness. We each grabbed a slice of pizza and talked. We talked about who had the best pizza in our hometown. We talked about cooking and our favorite restaurants. We talked about our favorite movies and our favorite getaway destinations. We talked about everything except the task that lay ahead of us. At one point, we came close to kissing when Gabby got up and said, "I think we should probably go to bed . . . I mean . . . sleep. I think we should go to sleep early tonight so we can get an early start tomorrow."

We both brushed our teeth and got into bed. This time Gabby got into bed fully clothed. I think she enjoyed teasing me before, but she seemed to want to put out the flames when things became more serious. I'm just not sure if it was my flame or hers that she wanted to put out.

I lay there thinking about how close I came to those soft, subtle lips. I thought about how I respected her for staying faithful to her boyfriend but also wished that she hadn't. I felt guilty for having erotic thoughts about someone other than my wife while at the same time knowing that Lisa was not my wife. Not anymore. Maybe not ever. Perhaps she was my wife, but I wasn't her husband, or vice versa. There were so many possibilities that I had a hard time wrapping my head around who I was.

Chapter 8

I woke up the next morning a little before sunrise. I noticed the light was on in the bathroom, and the door was closed. I didn't know how long Gabby had been awake, but it seemed like a good time for me to get up too. Plus, I had to pee. I got out of bed, slipped my pants on, and shuffled over to the bathroom door. "Good morning, Gabby," I said.

The door popped open a few inches, and I saw she had wet hair and a towel wrapped around her body. "Good morning. I will be out of here in five minutes if you need to use the bathroom."

"That's fine. I can wait." It wasn't fine because the urge to pee increased tenfold after getting out of bed, but I didn't want to tell her that.

True to her word, she came out five minutes later with her clothes on and her hair combed. She had not yet put on her makeup, but I thought she looked beautiful without it. We smiled at each other as we exchanged places but said nothing.

After relieving myself, I took a shower and got ready to go. When I was done brushing my teeth, shaving, and getting dressed, Gabby was almost ready to go. The sun was up by then, and I was anxious to get started.

"I've been thinking," I said. "I remember the water being on my right as we were driving to the boat, so I think we need to head south."

"That makes our job a little easier," Gabby said as we got into the car.

I searched for marinas on my phone after we got into the car and found four very close to each other, about five minutes away. The first was just a boat ramp, so we didn't bother getting out of the car. We did stop for the next one. We got out and walked down the docks looking for a boat with the word "Heaven" on it. It was a small marina, perhaps 30 boats, maybe more, but none had the word "Heaven" or any other divine name on it. The next two marinas also did not have the boat we were looking for.

By the time we were back on the road, my stomach was growling, and I said, "I think we should stop for breakfast soon. I'm getting hungry."

"I'm getting hungry, too," Gabby said. "Do you know a good place to eat around here?"

"I used to," I said, hoping it was still there. "You should turn right ahead and drive toward the beach. We need to go that way anyway."

After crossing the bridge and driving down the causeway to Clearwater Beach, we turned and headed down the coast for a block or two. There, directly across from the public beach, was the place I was looking for. It was a little bar and grill called "The Crotchety Crab" or something like that. I've eaten there a dozen times and could never remember the name. "Turn left here," I said.

Gabby turned down the nearest side street, and we parked the car and walked to the restaurant. Fortunately, they were still serving breakfast, and we could get a table outside. It was a bit chilly when we left the hotel, but now the temperature was just about perfect.

The menu had several alcohol options for breakfast, but I was never much of a drinker, so I just ordered an omelet and a coffee. I didn't drink coffee before college, but Lisa did, so I started drinking it with her. Now I feel like my morning is incomplete without it. Gabby ordered waffles and orange juice. While we waited for our food, we sat and watched all the beachgoers go by. We talked too. Gabby commented about how lucky I was to live near the beach.

"I was lucky," I said, with the stress on "was." "I don't think I would use that word to describe my current situation."

"Sorry. I know your life is pretty screwed up right now, but that won't last forever. A year from now, you will probably look back on this time as a great adventure."

"I hope you're right. I do feel like I am starting to accept who I am, even though I don't know who that is, and I could not have come this far without your help."

Gabby was about to say something when our waitress showed up with our drinks. "Here you go," she said. "Your food will be out shortly."

I thanked her, and as she walked away, Gabby said, "I have enjoyed our time together. I think I needed this almost as much as you."

"That makes me feel better," I said. "I just feel a little guilty because you have done so much for me, but I have been unable to do anything for you."

We were again interrupted by another woman, not our waitress, who put our food on the table and asked if we needed anything else. "No," I said. "Thank you."

When she walked away, I said, "Where were we?"

"We were about to enjoy our breakfast."

I sensed Gabby was uncomfortable with the topic, so I let it go. We finished breakfast without saying much except for some small talk. We put the top down on the Mustang when we left the restaurant because it was such a beautiful day.

We backtracked a few blocks to check out the marinas we had passed an hour earlier. We stopped first at the city's main marina on the island. We walked from one end to the other but did not find what we were looking for. We did see one boat called "Heaven's Bait," but it was a fishing charter boat. We then returned to the car and checked out the other three marinas in the area. None of the marinas had a boat with the word "Heaven" on it.

We continued south, checking out every marina on each island we came upon. After several hours I decided that we had gone too far. "It has to be closer than this," I said to Gabby. "We either missed it, it is no longer at the same marina, or the correct marina is on the mainland."

"We didn't miss anything," she said. "They may have moved it, but if they did, we would never find it, so let's assume it's on the mainland and check out those marinas."

It was well past lunch, and I was getting hungry, so I said, "I agree, but let's stop for a bite to eat first."

We were both anxious to find the boat before we had to go back to the hotel, so we decided to go through the first drive-through that we came across. That happened to be a McDonald's, which is not my favorite, but it was better than being hungry. We ordered a couple of cheeseburgers and fries and quickly ate them on our way to the next marina, which was not far.

The marina was relatively small, with about 40 slips, but a few of them were empty. We saw no sign of the boat we were looking for. It suddenly occurred to me that some empty slips probably were the home of boats that were out doing what boats do. "What if we missed the boat because it's out on the water?" I said.

"Unlikely," Gabby said. "Boats are expensive to operate. If you were in hiding, where would you get the money to go boating? I'm sure your father's accounts are being watched, so he needs to be frugal with the cash that he has."

I hadn't thought of that. "Good point," I said as we made our way back to the car.

We then drove to the last marina in the area. I was starting to feel like we needed to take a break, so when we parked the car, I said to Gabby, "We should call it a day after this one."

Gabby just nodded in agreement, and we both got out of the car. I believe the marina was called Bay Point Marina. It was a little bigger and more modern than most marinas we saw that day. It even had a restaurant and tiki bar as well as a store. We made our way to the boats and started reading names. About halfway down the first row of boats, I noticed a small cabin cruiser resembling Dr. Bill's boat. "This one," I said, pointing. "We are looking for a boat like this."

Gabby looked at the name and said, "Jill's Heave-Ho. That's a weird name."

"It sure is," I said. "Sometimes, I think boat owners compete. The weirdest name wins."

We continued looking, and when we got to the end and turned around, a thought occurred to me. "We need to go back to that Heave-Ho boat," I said as I picked up my pace.

Gabby raced to catch up to me. "What? What is it?"

When we reached the boat, I looked closely at the name and knew I was right. "Look! Look at the paint under the 'J' and the 'Ho.' Do you see how it is slightly whiter than the surrounding area?"

"Oh, my God!" Gabby said. "Someone changed the name."

"Exactly. This is Dr. Bill's boat. It used to be called 'Bill's Heaven.'"

We both looked around for people near us. I saw an older couple a few boats away, but they were both looking in another direction, so I said, "C'mon," and held out my hand. Gabby ignored it and stepped onto the boat. I followed her on.

Chapter 9

There was no sign that anyone was on the boat or evidence outside that anyone had been there recently. I tried the cabin door, but it was locked. I looked through the door, but there was no one in sight. From my vantage point, I could see a small stove and sink and a glass on the counter half filled with a clear liquid, probably water. I could also see a bed that was haphazardly made, like someone just quickly pulled the covers up.

I looked up and saw Gabby at the front of the boat peering through one of the cabin windows. "It looks like someone was here recently," I said. "What do you think?"

"I think we need to find someone who might know something. Let's talk to that couple over there."

"I was thinking the same thing."

The couple was three boats down on the same side of the dock. When we reached them, I said, "Hello."

They both turned to look at us, and the man said, "Good afternoon."

I estimated the couple to be in their late sixties or early seventies. They were white or Caucasian but had fairly dark skin, probably from spending their afternoons sitting in the sun.

"Do you folks live on your boat?" Gabby asked.

"Goin' on two years," the woman said. "Are you two interested in becoming liveaboards?"

"No," I said. "We are looking for my father. He is supposed to be staying on that boat, three boats down."

I pointed to the boat, and they both turned to look. The man shook his head and said, "A lot of people come up and down this dock. I can't say I remember anyone on that particular boat."

"I saw him," the woman said. "A man probably in his early fifties or so. I don't know. I didn't get a good look at his face, but he caught my eye because he seemed a bit overdressed, and he was pulling a large suitcase."

"When was that?" Gabby asked.

"Oh, a couple of weeks ago, maybe more, maybe less. I'm not sure," The woman said. "I think I've seen him a couple of times since then. Now that I think about it, I saw him leaving a couple of hours ago, but I wasn't paying attention, so that might have just been someone who looked similar."

"Thank you so much," I said. "You've been very helpful."

We walked back toward the car, and when we got far enough away, Gabby said, "If she is right, then he might have just gone out for dinner or supplies and will probably be back in a few hours, maybe even a few minutes."

"I agree," I said. "Let's go back to the car and do a stakeout like Starsky and Hutch."

"Like who? Gabby sad.

"Never mind," I said, realizing that my love of classic television was probably unusual for people our age. "Why don't you put the top up and keep an eye out from the car, and I will get us something to eat, okay?"

"That's fine," she said, "but you'll need some money." She pulled a twenty out of her purse and handed it to me. I hated relying on her for money and vowed to myself to make it up to her once I settled into a somewhat normal life.

I headed to the marina's restaurant and was pleased to find out that it was a casual restaurant, and they were happy to do takeout orders. I ordered two roast beef sandwiches, a large order of fries, and a couple of bottles of water. The order cost nearly the entire twenty dollars. Ten minutes later, I met Gabby in the car with the food.

"Did you see anything while I was gone?" I said after I got in the car.

"Not unless you call two drunk guys trying to decide who was least likely to kill someone driving home something," Gabby said.

"Well, I guess that would be something," I said as I handed her food to her.

Gabby unwrapped her sandwich and opened the bun. She seemed disappointed in my choice but said nothing and took a bite. When she finished chewing, she swallowed, put the sandwich down, and said, "You know, I think if your dad shows up, I should talk to him alone first. I think the sight of you might spook him."

"No, no, no!" I said, maybe too harshly, "I went through Hell looking for him, and I won't sit it out in the car. I'll tell you what, if he shows up, we will wait until he gets to the boat, and then we will go together to see him. He won't be able to run away then. Besides, I doubt he is much of a runner at his age. I know he wasn't five years ago."

Gabby had a look of resignation on her face and let out a small sigh before saying, "I guess that will work."

We finished our sandwiches, and Gabby asked, "Are you sure you want to do this? I mean, what if your father won't believe that you are his son? You may be better off not knowing than having to face that kind of rejection."

"I can handle it," I said. "I've had to adjust to many changes these last few days. I've come to accept who I am and who I am not. Let me rephrase that. I still feel like I am having some kind of identity crisis, but I know I need to deal with it, and I will."

"I don't doubt that you will," Gabby said. "I just don't want you to get hurt."

Just then, we noticed a middle-aged man walking down the dock carrying two bags that I assumed were groceries. Even from our distance, I could tell it was Dad. "That's him," I said excitedly.

"Give him a minute to get to the boat," Gabby said.

"We'll walk slow," I said as I got out of the car.

"Wait for me!" Gabby yelled and got out of the car to join me.

We walked together, and I could see Dad stepping onto the boat when we reached the dock. We continued walking, and when we got about halfway to the boat, Gabby grabbed my arm and said, "Shit!"

"What is it?" I said.

"I forgot to lock the car, and my purse is in there," she said. "I'll be right back. Don't do anything stupid while I'm gone."

"Okay," I said as she started walking back to the car. "I'll wait until you come back before doing something stupid."

I turned back to the boat and decided what the hell. I quickly walked the remaining distance, took a deep breath, then stepped aboard the boat. The cabin door was closed, so I knocked three times and then called out, "Hello! Mr. Neumann?"

I heard some noise in the cabin, and then the door opened slightly, and a hand came out holding a handgun. Then the door opened a little further, and my father emerged, pointing the gun at me.

I quickly raised my hands and said, "Dad! Don't shoot!"

He looked at me puzzled and said, "Dad? Who the hell are you, and what are you doing on my boat?"

"Please, give me a minute to explain," I said. "This is going to be hard to believe, but it's me, Alex," I said. "I know if anyone can believe it, it would be you."

"Is this a joke? I know my son, and you are not him," he said.

"Five years ago, Lisa and I met you at your lab because we wanted to tell you Lisa was pregnant," I said. "You had just made some kind of breakthrough and needed my help, so I let you put me into that device of yours where you copied my brain. Scott Parker then put my brain into this body, or my memories, anyway. He implied you were working for the Russians and said he needed my help to find you before someone more dangerous found you, but I escaped and tracked you here."

Dad had a shocked look on his face and said softly, "Holy shit." He then raised the gun higher and said, "Wait a minute. How do I know you are not working for Parker as some kind of bounty hunter or whatever you call it? This would be standard operating procedure for them."

"Do you remember when I was in the fourth grade and that bully, Jack something or other, was taking my lunch money?" I asked. "I don't know how you did it, but you dug up dirt on the kid and found out he was seeing a therapist. You got a business card from the therapist and wrote on the card, 'I will tell everyone.' You told me to give it to the bully the next time he demanded money. I did that, and he never bothered me again."

"The kid's name was Jack Williams. His mother brought him in to see me because she was convinced his behavior was caused by a neurological disorder," Dad said. "He was really just an asshole, and I referred him to a psychologist."

He lowered the gun and said, "Why did we name you Alex?"

"I was named in honor of Mom's sister, Alexa. She died in a car accident a couple of months before I was born."

"It is you, Alex. I don't believe it. Of course, knowing Scott Parker, I shouldn't be surprised. Come on in," he said as he pushed the door all the way open.

I followed him inside the cabin. He set the gun down on a small table, turned to me, and said, "I knew that this was Parker's ultimate plan, but I never expected it to happen to you. I just wanted a way to reintroduce lost memories into dementia patients, but Parker, it turns out, wanted so much more. How did you get away from him? How did you find me?"

"I had a lot of help from your friend, Gabby," I said.

"Gabby?" he said, with a confused look on his face. "I hope you don't mean Gabriella."

"Yes," I said, "that's her real name."

"Shit!" he said. "She's Parker's girlfriend. Where is she now?"

"I'm right here," came a voice from behind me.

Chapter 10

The voice sounded like Gabby, but she had no accent. I turned to look, and it was Gabby. She was holding a gun and moving it back and forth, pointing it first at me and then at Dad and back at me again. "Alex, pick up that gun by the barrel and throw it to me."

I could not believe that I had been so thoroughly duped. I thought about grabbing the gun and trying to get a shot off, but I never used a gun before and would probably just get shot in the attempt. I reached for the gun, and Gabby said, "Slowly!" I slowly picked up the gun and tossed it at her feet.

"I notice your accent is gone," I said. "Is anything you told me true?"

"Not much," she said. "I was born in Los Angeles. My father is a dentist, and my mother is an insurance agent. I do have a boyfriend like I told you, and I was interested in finding your father. Those things were true."

"I should have known," I said. "Scott Parker is your boyfriend. How could I have been so stupid?"

"You're a man," she said and picked up the other gun and pointed it at Dad. "Now, I need the software you stole from the lab."

"I stole nothing from the lab," Dad said. "After discovering what Parker and General Rafferty were up to, I simply destroyed it so you couldn't use it."

"What were they up to?" I asked.

"Enough talking. Now give me what I want, or I'll shoot him," Gabby said, referring to me.

"Why should I care?" Dad said. "I don't even know this man."

"Of course you do," Gabby said. "He's your son. I'm sure you already had your little reunion before I showed up. Plus, now you have two sons, and I can arrange to have your real son shot, too, if you don't cooperate."

Dad looked at me and then at Gabby. After a few seconds, he said, "Okay, I'll get it."

"No!" Gabby said. "Not you, him," and turned her head toward me."

I looked at Dad. He looked at me. After a short pause, he said, "It's in the coffee jar above the sink."

I opened the cabinet and pulled out a glass jar with coffee in it. I removed the lid and reached for a spoon that was on the drying rack. I put the spoon in the coffee and rooted around until I felt something. I then pulled it to the surface. It was a thumb drive. I took it out, blew the coffee off it, and held it up for Gabby to see.

Gabby looked at Dad and said, "Where's your laptop?"

"I didn't bring it with me," Dad said.

"Bullshit!" Gabby said. "We went to your house. You didn't leave it behind."

Dad hesitated for a few seconds and then pointed to my left, "Bottom drawer," he said.

I opened the bottom drawer. Inside was a laptop sitting on top of several dish towels. I removed it and started to hand it to Gabby, but she said, "Put it on the table and turn it on."

I did as she said and pushed aside several papers held in place by a glass paperweight resembling a mini fishbowl with little goldfish inside. Once I had the computer up and running, I inserted the thumb drive. It beeped, and then a window opened with several folders and a program labeled "MindMapper."

"Run the program," Gabby said.

I looked at Dad, who nodded. I double-clicked the icon, and the program opened. It was a basic user interface. It was far from anything you would expect from commercial software, just white text on a dark blue background with the word "MindMapper" on the top and several buttons with labels like home, edit, help, etc. At the bottom was a grayed-out button that said "Start" and red text underneath that said, "Not Connected."

"That's it," Gabby said, "Give it to me."

I pulled the thumb drive out and tossed it to her. I was hoping that trying to catch it with a gun in each hand would distract her, but she did not attempt to catch it. Instead, the thumb drive just hit her and fell to the floor.

"Nice try," she said as she put Dad's gun in her purse, slowly squatted down, and picked up the thumb drive while keeping the other gun pointed at me. She then dropped the card in her purse and pulled out her phone.

"You got what you came for," I said. I was about to say something about not needing us anymore but decided that might be a bad idea, so I stopped talking.

Gabby did not answer. Instead, she dialed a number and held the phone to her ear. After a few seconds, she said, "I have it." After a few more seconds, she said, "Consider it done," and hung up.

She put the phone back in her purse, looked at me, and said, "I had fun on our little adventure, but it is over now." With that, she pointed the gun at Dad and pulled the trigger.

"No!" I screamed, and without thinking, I picked up the paperweight and threw it. At that moment, everything seemed to go in slow motion. I watched Gabby turn the gun on me just as the glass paperweight hit her square on her forehead. She dropped like a rock.

I knelt to check on Dad. He was bleeding from the center of his chest and seemed to have trouble breathing. "Hang on, Dad," I said. "I'll get help."

As I started to get up, he grabbed my arm and said, almost in a whisper, "No, it's too late for that." He struggled to get words out but finally said what sounded like "sugar" before he stopped breathing.

"Dad!" I yelled. "Dad, stay with me!"

I checked for a pulse but couldn't find one, so I started CPR. I knew it was hopeless, but I had to try. After a couple of minutes, I just slumped back and gave up. I wanted to just sit there and cry, but I had no time for that. I couldn't wait for the police because I would have difficulty explaining who I was. I also had no idea how, but I needed to make Parker pay for Dad's death, and I knew the police would be of no help.

I thought about what Dad could have meant by "sugar." Then it hit me. I opened the cabinet where I found the coffee, and there, on the same shelf, I found an identical container, but this one had sugar in it. I opened it and felt around with my fingers. There was something there. I pulled it out. It was a piece of paper folded several times. I unfolded it and saw it was a letter with a key taped to the bottom. I had no time to read it, so I stuck it in my pocket.

I then got busy. I checked on Gabby. She was breathing but unconscious. She was still holding the gun, so I figured it would be easy for the cops to figure it out, but I'm sure they would also wonder why she was unconscious. I found a towel, wiped my fingerprints from the paperweight, and placed it in Dad's hand. I then put it back where I picked it up from. With any luck, they will think Dad hit her with it when she shot him.

I wiped down everything that I touched. I left the guns but took the memory card, keys, cash, and phone from Gabby's purse. I also took Dad's laptop and charger. I left the credit card and a few dollars. I also put the phone Gabby gave me into her purse. I didn't want the police to think something was missing and conclude a third person was involved, although they would possibly come to that conclusion eventually.

My main concern was the older couple on the other boat. If they heard the gunshot, the police could already be on the way. I stepped off the boat and casually walked in their direction, but they were not there. There were no lights on below, so they must have gone out for dinner or something. In any case, I thought the cops might talk to them and learn that I was there with Gabby, but I would be long gone by then.

I walked down to the dockmaster's office and told the guy there that I saw a crazy woman with a gun at the Jill's Heave-Ho boat and that he should call the police. I walked away as he picked up the phone.

After driving for a couple of blocks, I pulled into the parking lot of a pharmacy and took out Gabby's phone. It was locked, but I saw her open it when we were in the hotel. I remembered because the unlock pattern was the letter G. I opened it and read her text messages. The only recent messages were to Parker. They were all updates on our status.

I typed, "It's done. Can't talk now. Heading back." I knew Parker would know the truth once the police arrested Gabby, but that would be hours away. I figured the longer he was in the dark, the better.

I took out the letter from Dad. On the outside, it said, "If found, please give to Alex Neuman." I unfolded it and started reading.

"Dear Alex, if you are reading this letter, I am probably dead. I have been thinking a lot lately about how I failed you as a dad. When your mom was sick, and even after she died, I immersed myself in my work instead of my family. I was trying to make things better for others when I should have been trying to make things better for you and for us. I am so sorry about that.

I recently found myself in trouble after discovering the real goal of my work at Parker Biosystems. I did not have enough proof to go to the police, so I did the only thing I could think to do. I took away what Scott Parker needed to accomplish his plan. I have been working on a way to expose the truth. I fear that you and your family will be in danger until Parker gets what he wants or is arrested and put in jail.

I left you a key. I'm sure you will know what it is for. Do not attempt to take down Parker yourself. He is too dangerous. Find a place to lie low and, if you want to, investigate him from a safe place. You have always been good at that computer stuff. I know you will think of something. Good luck and be careful. Love Dad."

I had a pretty good idea what the key was for, but that would have to wait until tomorrow. I was tired and could not risk returning to the hotel. I went into the pharmacy, used their bathroom, and bought a bottle of water on the way out.

I quickly got back on the road and drove until I found an empty parking lot. I parked the car in the far corner, put the seat back, and tried to get some sleep. Sleeping in a car was never something I did well, and this was no exception. I was awake for quite a while, but after more than an hour, I finally dozed off.

Chapter 11

I awoke to knocking on my window. It was a cop. Shit! I looked at my watch. 4:58 a.m. I rolled down my window.

"Is everything okay?" he asked. "Do you need assistance?"

"I'm sorry, officer," I said. "No. I'm okay. I drove down here from Virginia to see my dad, but my wallet was stolen, and I have no money for gas. I'm waiting for my dad to wire money to me."

"Unfortunately, you can't wait here, son," he said. "You'll have to move along."

"Of course," I said. "I'm sorry. I'll leave now." I was thankful he didn't want to look me up, so I quickly rolled up my window and drove away before he changed his mind.

I drove back toward Dunedin and saw a Waffle House that was open. I needed to kill some time and thought I could eat an early breakfast.

I brought the laptop inside and looked for clues in Dad's files but found nothing useful. I did find several hundred photos dating back to when Dad was a child up to when Lisa and I were married. There were several photos of Mom and Dad when they were young and many of me when I was a baby and toddler. It felt good to reminisce, but after a while, I realized I had more important things to do.

After more than two hours and several cups of coffee, I decided I had killed enough time. I needed to go to the one place that I did not want to go back to. I was not going to be welcome there. That was for sure.

About fifteen minutes later, I pulled into my driveway, or, to be technically correct, the driveway of Alex Neumann. I sat in the car for a minute, trying to decide what I was going to say. When nothing came to me, I just got out and headed to the front door.

Someone must have seen or heard me pull in because as I approached the house, the door opened slightly. Alex peered out, pointed a finger at me, and said, "You killed my father, you son of a bitch! I'm calling the police!"

I stepped forward and put my foot in the door just as he closed it and said, "Wait! The woman I was with used me. I admit I was stupid. It's my fault. I am sick about it. I thought she wanted to help Dad, but she just wanted something from him. When she got it, she shot him. She tried to shoot me too, but I knocked her out before she could. That is why she was caught. She is working for Scott Parker, and since I have what they are looking for now, my life is in danger too. I need your help. Please."

Alex relaxed his hold on the door and let it open slightly. "Dad?" he said. "Who are you, and how did you find my father in the first place?"

"Give me a few minutes, and I will explain everything," I said.

He thought for several long seconds and said, "Okay, but I need your keys first."

"My keys?" I said.

"Your car keys," he said. "Give me your keys, and I will talk to you."

He must have noticed the confused look on my face, so he said, "Look, I still don't trust you. You are less likely to cause problems if you can't drive away. Also, if I take your keys and then have to call the police, it will be harder for you to get away. So, showing me trust will go a long way toward me trusting you."

I couldn't argue with that logic and wondered how I got so smart. I reached into my pocket and handed over the keys.

Alex took the keys and called Lisa, who appeared behind him a few seconds later. Seeing her again filled me with emotion. I wanted to push through the door and take her in my arms, but I knew that would do nothing but land me in jail. "Here," he said. "Take these and lock the door behind me. If

68

you hear anything unusual, call the police." He quickly stepped outside and closed the door before she had time to protest.

"Okay, let's hear it," he said.

"Do you remember getting your head scanned at your father's lab about five years ago?" I said.

"Sure, that was when my father was first able to map a person's memory with his invention," Alex said.

"Do you know why he went to work for Scott Parker?" I said.

"I remember his goal was to restore lost memories after a person had lost a significant portion of their memories from Alzheimer's disease or other types of dementia," he said. "He could not accomplish that with his limited resources at the university. I tried to talk him out of it. I thought he was selling his soul to the devil, but he wouldn't listen. He kept going on about how many people he would be able to help."

"Did you know they built a machine that could implant memories into the human brain?" I said.

"The last time I talked to my father, he said they were close, but that was all I heard. He disappeared shortly after that," Alex said.

"What I am about to tell you will sound very hard to believe, but it is true," I said. "Your dad discovered that Scott Parker had other plans for the device. Those plans were bad enough to prompt your father to destroy the software needed to record people's memories and disappear. He was able to corrupt the software that reads and records memories, but he was not able to destroy the machine that rewrites a person's brain.

Parker recovered the brain scans your father took that day five years ago, but only one of them was helpful to him: yours."

"You are right," Alex said. "That sounds very far-fetched. And why would my brain scan be important anyway?"

"Because only you could help them find your father," I said.

Alex thought about it for a few seconds, then looked at me and said, "Wait a minute. You're not telling me that you are . . ."

"That is exactly what I am telling you," I said. "I am you. Scott Parker told me that your memories were implanted into this body. He told me this body is a clone. The plan was to grow physically superior humans and implant the memories of elite special forces soldiers. Imagine taking the best of the best and duplicating them en masse."

"Cloning humans is illegal," Alex said.

"Do you think that ever stopped our government before?" I said. "I think maybe this is what Dad discovered."

"I'm not convinced, and I am also uncomfortable with you calling him 'Dad,'" he said.

"How do you think I found him in the first place?" I asked. "I used your memory of going out on Dr. Bill's boat."

"That's just crazy," he said. "I don't know how you knew that, but it doesn't prove anything. "

'Okay," I said. "Ask me anything that only you know from before five years ago."

"Tell me about the first fight I was ever in."

"I don't remember, and neither do you. Ask me a real question."

"Okay. How did I break my foot as a child?"

"You got a ladder and climbed onto the roof. You were convinced that you could use your bed sheet as a parachute. You were wrong."

"Yeah, that was embarrassing," Alex said, "but I'm sure I told someone that. Tell me, what was my favorite class in high school?"

"Science," I said. "We probably should have got into science instead of computers."

Alex looked at me in astonishment. "That's right," he said slowly, "but I like computers too."

"You are good at computers, and it pays the bills, but you have no passion for it," I said.

Alex thought for a moment and said, "I suppose you are right about that too. It has always been just a job. I should have followed my passion, but I thought computers would be a more stable career choice. Okay, how did I get this scar on the back of my hand?" He showed me the small scar on his hand that was hard to see. It had faded somewhat since the last time I really looked at it.

"You were trying to make friends with a goose when you were very young, maybe four years old," I said. "The goose turned out to be not so friendly."

"I'm starting to think that maybe you aren't crazy," he said. "Tell me one more. How did Lisa tell me about our first child?"

"She surprised you with a nice, candlelit dinner."

"What did she cook for dinner?"

"She didn't cook anything. She ordered Chinese food."

"That's incredible," Alex said. "I never told anyone that."

"It is incredible. You are right about that. If I wanted to lie to you, I would have told you something more believable," I said.

"Okay, I believe you."

"So, will you help me?"

"I will do what I can. What do you need from me?"

I pulled the key out of my pocket and held it up. "Does Dad still have a safety deposit box at your bank?"

"I believe so. Where did you get that?"

I pulled the note out of my pocket and handed it to Alex. "The key was attached to the letter."

Alex read the letter and then handed it back to me. "Keep it. Dad wrote it for you," I said.

"There are certain protocols that the bank must follow after the death of a customer, but I am friends with the manager. I think he will let me in," Alex said.

"You're friends with Martin? The guy who said so everyone could hear that he couldn't believe someone as hot as Lisa would go out with a guy like you?"

"No, that asshole was fired years ago, not long after the brain scan, I think. The new manager transferred from another location. You wouldn't know him.

He pulled his phone out of his pocket and hit a number on his contact list. After a few seconds, he said, "Hi Terry. It's Alex. Yes, thank you. It was a shock. Listen, is Frank around? Okay, thanks."

Alex hung up and said, "He's busy and will call me back in five minutes. In the meantime, I'll get my keys, and we can head to the bank. I prefer you to come with me. I know how you feel about Lisa, and quite frankly, I don't want you anywhere near her."

I understood his concern. Who would be a greater threat to a happy marriage than someone exactly like you but bigger and stronger? "No worries," I said. "I have already made peace with the fact that I am not you and have no intention of hurting my former self."

As soon as we got into Alex's car, the phone rang. "This is my boss, so don't say anything," he said.

He pressed a button on the steering wheel and said, "Hi, Frank. Thanks for calling me back."

A loud, raspy voice came through the speakers, "Hi, Alex. I'm so sorry to hear about your father. What can I do for you?"

"Thanks, Frank. I need a favor. My father has a safety deposit box at the bank, and I need to look inside it."

"You know I can't allow that, Alex. You need a death certificate and proof that you are the legal heir."

"I understand, but you know my father is dead. It was all over the news. You also know my mother is dead, and I have no siblings. It is important. What is in there could be evidence in his murder."

"I thought they caught the woman who did it."

"They did, but she was working for someone very powerful. If there is evidence in that box, the sooner we get it, the better."

"What the hell was your father into?"

"That's what I am trying to find out, Frank. Can you help?"

"Just a minute," Frank said, and we heard him tapping on his keyboard. After about fifteen seconds, he said, "It looks like you are already authorized on his account. It's recent too. Your father added you about two weeks ago. You didn't know this?"

"No, I didn't," Alex said. "Thanks for your help, Frank."

The drive to Tampa was a bit awkward at first. I wasn't exactly sure what to say to myself, so I asked questions about the last five years. Alex told me about his promotion at work. He told me about his kids and when the baby was due. He told me the boy was named Steven and the girl was named Elizabeth. He told me about their plan to buy a bigger house within the next couple of years. He also told me that he only occasionally heard from Dad since he took the job with Parker and that it had been two years since they saw each other in person. I felt bad that I missed all of it and thought if I had been there, I would have made a better effort to see Dad. Then I realized I was there and didn't make that effort.

When we got to the bank, Alex said, "I think it would be better if you waited in the car."

"That's fine," I said. "I understand."

Alex went into the bank but left the car running, presumably so I could keep the air conditioner on while I waited. I turned on the radio and flipped through the stations until a news story caught my attention. "The suspect in the murder of Dr. Bernard Neumann was released on bail early this morning. She is charged with a firearms violation, but she so far has not been charged with murder due to lack of evidence. Her attorney insists that Dr. Neumann attacked his client after she confronted him about stolen material from Parker Biosystems, where he worked. Her attorney claims that her gun when off when Mr. Neumann hit her on the head with a paperweight. According to police, she was found unconscious at the scene. In other news . . .

I turned the radio off. I needed to think. If Gabby was out already, they would be looking for me sooner than planned.

Alex returned a few minutes later with a hard drive in his hand. "This was the only thing in the box," he said. "Maybe there is evidence on it. We can take it back to my house and look at it."

"There's no time for that now," I said. "I just learned Gabby was released from custody this morning. They will be looking for me soon and may go through you to find me."

"Shit! What are we going to do now?" asked Alex.

"We are not going to do anything," I said. "You are going to take your family away from home for a few days. Tell no one where you are going. Keep your phones at home, and for God's sake, don't use your credit cards."

"What are you going to do?" Alex asked.

"I haven't figured that out yet."

"There must be something I can do."

"I could use some cash," I said. "Whatever you can spare, but make sure you have plenty for yourself."

Since we were already at his bank, Alex went back in and came out with a wad of cash. He peeled off ten fifty-dollar bills and handed them to me. "I wish I could do more to help," he said.

"This is enough, but I could use a couple of things at your house," I said.

When we got back to Alex's house, he went inside and came out with a hard drive adapter cable and a pair of Ray-Ban sunglasses. I bought them when I was still in high school. I was surprised he still had them. "Are you sure you don't need anything else?" he said.

"This will do," I said. "By the way, do you still have our old Yahoo email?"

"I do, but I never use it anymore."

"That's good. It probably won't be monitored. I will update you there if I have any news, but it won't be soon. Remember, stay off any electronic devices for a while unless you are one hundred percent secure."

I got in the car and drove away. After a few blocks, I pulled into a strip mall, parked the car, looked up a number, and dialed. When the call was answered, I said, "Can I speak with Michael Hansen, please?"

Chapter 12

I dropped Gabby's phone into the nearest trash can and settled in for the long drive back to Virginia. I had enough cash for gas, but I wasn't sure how long it would last after I got there. I also knew there was a chance I wouldn't get there. With Parker's influence, the car was possibly already listed as stolen. I hoped that since Mustangs are so common, it would be like looking for a particular needle in a haystack full of needles. I just needed to make sure I didn't do anything to draw attention to myself, like speeding.

I wanted to see what was on the hard drive, but I also wanted to get a good distance away before anyone started looking for me. I waited until I crossed into Georgia and then stopped at the first gas station I saw off the highway. I filled the tank and used the restroom. The place had a sandwich shop inside, so I purchased an Italian sub sandwich and a bottle of water. I drove to a far corner of the parking lot and ate the sandwich. When I finished, I pulled out the laptop.

I connected the drive to the computer and opened the file explorer. It contained hundreds of folders, all labeled only with numbers, except for one. One folder was labeled "0000 Start Here." I assumed it was labeled that way, so it would appear first. I opened it. Inside was a single video file labeled only with a date and time. I double-clicked on the file and hit play when the video player opened.

It looked like security camera footage of the inside of a lab, but the angle was low, and I could see part of a desk or table like it was taken with a laptop's webcam. I saw the door open on the left side of the screen, and Parker came into the room. He looked left and then right and then headed straight to the camera.

He started looking through drawers and then sat down and looked slightly down, confirming that it was indeed a webcam. He was looking for something on the computer. I wished the video also included what was on the screen, but it didn't. After several minutes General Rafferty walked in and stood behind Parker. "Did you find anything yet?" he said.

"Nothing yet," said Parker.

"Check his email," said Rafferty. "If he knows something, he might have tried to tell someone."

"That was the first thing I looked at," Parker said. "Even if he knew something, who would he tell? What would he say? People would think he's crazy. Besides, nobody knows what our machine can do."

"Still, I don't like that he has been asking questions," Rafferty said. "If even a hint of what we're planning gets out, we can kiss the presidency goodbye. I think we need to get rid of him."

"We still need him," Parker said. "Once we confirm that the machine is working properly, we can arrange a little accident for our friend."

"Excuse me, General," came a voice in the background. "Your wife is waiting downstairs for you."

The general turned and exposed a security guard standing behind him at the door. That security guard looked just like me.

"How much of that conversation did you hear?" the general asked.

"I heard nothing, sir," he said. "I just walked in."

At that point, the video reached the ten-minute mark and ended. It must have been set to record in ten-minute chunks. I wanted to see what happened to my other self, but I suppose Dad did not find that important at the time and didn't copy it. I wondered why he was recording in the first place. He must have had trust issues, and I could certainly see why.

I copied the video onto the laptop and disconnected the hard drive. I put the drive in the glove compartment and put the laptop under the seat. I then sat there for a while, thinking about what I had just seen. It was a lot to take in. I understood now why Dad did what he did. I wondered what they meant by kissing the presidency goodbye. Could they possibly replace the president? What a scary thought that was. Parker's mind in the president of the United States would be a disaster for the country. Worse, Parker and Rafferty could get their minds implanted into the heads of the leaders of every government agency or all the top generals, or both. They could even infiltrate foreign governments.

Chapter 13

I got back on the road and just drove. I kept the radio off and tried to think about what to do next. Nothing came to mind. I knew I couldn't wait for Parker or Gabby to find me. I needed to be proactive. Unfortunately, what I could do was eluding me at that moment. I wasn't a special agent or a cop. I had no skills in investigations.

I drove until I could barely keep my eyes open and pulled into a rest stop. I parked far from the building and went inside to use the washroom. I bought a bottle of water and a bag of potato chips and checked the map. I was somewhere in the middle of South Carolina. I then went back to the car. Sleeping in the back seat didn't seem like it would be comfortable or even possible, so I sat in the driver's seat and leaned it back as far as it would go. It didn't take long for me to fall asleep this time.

I woke up when the sun rose above the tree line and shone in my eyes. I looked around, and everything seemed normal. I had to pee, so I headed to the bathroom. When I came out, I saw a state trooper slowly driving past my car. I stopped and watched, but the vehicle continued and parked in front of me. I casually walked toward the car. When I got halfway there, I bent down to tie my shoe while I glanced back to see what the trooper was doing. He was walking toward the bathroom. I guessed his bladder was his main concern at the time.

I decided not to wait for him to come out. I got in the car and quickly drove away, but not too quickly. I checked my rearview for a while and then relaxed.

By noon I was getting close to my destination. I wanted to push on, but I was hungry. A small bag of potato chips was not a very good breakfast. I wanted some real food, so I pulled off the highway and found a mom-and-pop restaurant near a few fast-food places. I ordered a grilled chicken sandwich. I probably could have gotten a grilled chicken sandwich from one of the fast-food places, but this somehow felt different.

I got out the address Michael Hansen gave me and thought about what to expect. I considered what I would say. So many scenarios crossed my mind. I decided I would have to wing it, which I have been doing a lot lately.

When I finished eating, I paid the bill and continued heading north. After about forty-five minutes, I was in Fredericksburg and reached my exit. The car didn't have navigation, and I did not keep Gabby's phone for fear of being tracked, so I had to follow directions carefully as people did in the old days. The place was not too far from the exit, and I soon reached the apartment complex I was looking for. It was a new-looking place with big flags at the entrance that said, "Now Leasing." Close to the front was apartment 134. I pulled into a guest spot two spots down from a Fredericksburg Police car. It was actually an SUV that said "Canine Unit" on the back. I assumed the officer lived in one of the apartments, so I decided it wasn't worth abandoning my plan. I also had no reason to believe anyone knew I was in Fredericksburg.

After sitting in the car for a minute trying to work up my courage, I finally got out and walked up to the door. I hesitated for a second but then knocked three times. I waited. I waited some more. I knocked again. Suddenly I heard a dog bark behind me. I turned to see a beautiful blond woman wearing a police uniform and holding a large German Shepherd on a leash. I recognized something familiar about her and briefly wondered who she looked like, but I had other things to think about after she deliberately let go of the dog's leash. The dog lunged at me. After everything I had been through, I thought a police dog would now finish me off. Instead, the dog put his paws on my chest and stretched to lick my face.

"Bruno! Down!" the woman said after about ten or fifteen seconds, and the dog quickly lay at my feet.

The policewoman then walked up to me and threw her arms around me. "I'm so happy you came back, John," she said in my ear before pulling away. She then slapped me hard across my left cheek. "What the hell happened to you?" she yelled. "Where have you been? Why didn't you call? I thought you were dead!"

I assumed the policewoman was Annette Hansen and said, "Can we go inside and talk?"

She looked at me for a few seconds and then bent down to pick up Bruno's leash. "C'mon boy!" she said. Bruno got up, and the two of them walked into the apartment. She left the door open, so I took that as an invitation to come in.

I walked into an immaculate apartment. To the left was a large living room with a sectional sofa against the window and the left wall. A large television hung on the wall opposite the window. It was at least 65 inches, maybe bigger. In front of the television was an exercise bike. I assumed she had a biking video that played during her exercises.

"Can I get you something to drink?" she said.

"Water, if you don't mind," I said.

She turned to walk into the kitchen, which was on the other side of the wall where the television was. She was beautiful. She reminded me a lot of Lisa. I imagined her in tight workout clothes riding that exercise bike. After about a minute, she returned with a glass of water.

"Have a seat," she said as she handed me the glass. I sat at the end of the sofa, near the door. She had no coffee table, but she did have a small end table on each side of the sofa. I took a drink of water and set the glass on a coaster on the end table. Annette put her right leg on the cushion next to me as she sat so she could look at me better. Bruno sat on the floor on the other side and stared at me. He was wearing a vest that said, "Fredericksburg Police." I felt like I was being interrogated.

"Ann," I said.

"Ann?" she said. "You've never called me that before. What happened to Annie? What is going on with you?"

"Annie," I said. "What I am about to tell you is hard to believe. Impossible, really. I'm asking you to please, please, keep an open mind.

"I'm listening."

"I'm not John. I just look like him."

Annie interrupted me, saying, "Okay, I don't need to listen to your nonsense excuses. You should go now. When you are ready to tell me what is really going on, I will be here."

"Wait a second!" I said. "You were going to keep an open mind here."

"You said that, not me."

"Please, give me a chance to explain. If you still want to kick me out after hearing the entire story, I will leave and not bother you again. But I hope to convince you because I need your help. I don't know what else to do."

"Fine. Let's hear your story."

"My name is Alex Neumann. At least that is what I remember," I said. "I was born and raised in Florida, not far from Tampa. My father was a neurologist. My mother suffered from early-onset Alzheimer's disease. My dad was obsessed with finding a cure, but he was too late. He continued his work after Mom died. He found a way to record people's memories. He hoped to be able to take those memories and implant them back into his patients after their memories degraded to a certain point. It would not have extended their lives, but it would have allowed them to be functional for much longer."

I could see Annie was listening like she was genuinely interested, so I continued. "Implanting memories back into a person's brain is much more difficult than extracting them, not that either is easy. Dad couldn't do it by himself, so he hooked up with a guy named Scott Parker of Parker Biosystems."

"I know about them, John. You worked there," Annie said.

"Yes, I pieced that together. I'll get to that. Anyway, they already had the resources and experience connecting human minds to machines."

"You did tell me about some of their projects, but you never mentioned anything about memories."

"John probably didn't know about that. It was probably a secret project."

"You keep talking about yourself in the third person," Annie said. "It's weird."

"Let me get to that," I said. "Anyway, five years ago, when my dad made his first breakthrough, he asked me to allow him to scan my brain so he could test his device. He also scanned himself, one of his students, and my wife."

"Your wife?"

"I'll get to that, too. Several days ago, I woke up in a room inside Parker Biosystems. In my mind, a very short time had passed, but in reality, I had lost five years. I also lost myself. I woke up in a body that was not mine. I'm not this good-looking. Parker, and a General Rafferty, told me this body is a clone."

"Rafferty?" Annie said. "You've talked about him before."

"Maybe John talked about him, but I didn't."

"C'mon, John. That is a ridiculous story. I know you're no clone."

"What makes you so sure?"

"The scar on your arm, for one thing," she said as she pointed to my right arm. "You were grazed by a bullet in Afghanistan. Are you going to tell me you don't remember that? I don't know much about cloning, but I know scars are not embedded in your DNA."

I looked down, and there, just above my elbow, was a scar about two inches long. "Holy shit," I said. "Do you have a mirror?"

"In the bathroom," she said, pointing down the hall.

I went into the bathroom, took off my shirt, and carefully examined my body. Annie watched me from the doorway. "Do I have any other war wounds?"

"I don't know if you would call it a war wound but look at the back of your right hand."

I looked at my hand but didn't see anything at first. I then noticed a thin scar across the two middle fingers near the knuckles. "How did I get this?" I asked.

"You punched the class bully in eighth grade. You learned a valuable lesson that day. Never punch a kid wearing braces. At least not in the mouth."

"I can't picture a bully with braces."

"They come in all different varieties," she said.

I realized then that the clone story was a lie. I was no clone. I was John Thomas, and Annie was my fiancée. "Oh, my God! You're right, Annie," I said. "I really am John. The clone story was a lie."

I think my genuine surprise was somewhat convincing, and she said, "You honestly believe what you are telling me, don't you?"

I nodded. "Yes, I do."

"Could this be the result of some kind of brainwashing?" she asked.

"No. I have over two decades of memories. Those couldn't have been brainwashed into me."

"I want to believe you, John, but I need more."

"I have more," I said. I put on my shirt and walked past her and out to the car. When I returned, I had the laptop. The two of us sat on the sofa, and I brought up the video I had copied to it. Annie watched intently. When it was over, I could see it had visibly shaken her.

"Have you shown this to anyone else?"

"No. I may need leverage later. Besides, it's not proof of anything specific. It just shows that they are up to no good."

"That is some unbelievable shit," she said. "What did he mean when he said, 'lose the presidency?'"

"I don't know for sure, but I suspect they have a plan in the works to scan the president's brain. Maybe they will convince him he could live forever. It would be tempting for anyone. Once they have him in the machine, they can reverse the process and implant Parker's memories into the president's mind. The Secret Service wouldn't even know anything happened if Parker was prepared for it."

Annie had a shocked look on her face. "So, if this device works as you say, Parker could soon be running this country, and nobody would know? That's a scary thought."

"Don't worry," I said. "I have the program they need to accomplish their goals, and I have no intention of giving it to them."

"I'm sorry for being so angry with you before, but you must admit it is a crazy story. I will trust you on this. I have always trusted you, and I'm not going to stop now. It is very scary to know humans are now capable of taking over the minds of other humans."

"I agree. It's very scary."

So, tell me, what do you remember from John's life?"

"Nothing, as far as I can tell," I said. "I'm sorry. I wish I could tell you something different, but I can't. I wondered what happened to John at the end of the video, and now I know. They replaced him with me."

"Listen, John," she said. "I'm sorry. I mean Alex."

"No, don't be sorry. I think it is time I left Alex behind. I am John, after all. I need to have my own life, and I think I found it. I hope that doesn't seem disrespectful to the old John. I do respect him and know that I could never replace him, but I can continue living for him if that makes any sense."

"I think I understand," Annie said. "I cried many nights thinking that you were dead. Now that you are here but not the man I knew, I don't know how I feel. I am sad that the John I know is gone, but he is also still here. You are still here. That somehow makes it less painful."

I nodded but said nothing. I knew Annie needed time to adjust to what had happened.

"Listen," she said again. "I want to help you, but right now, I must go to work. You are welcome to stay here if you want to. I won't be home until after eight, though."

"I appreciate that," I said. "You should know that I have not told you the entire story yet, and people will be looking for me. I don't want to put you in danger."

"I can take care of myself," she said. "When I get home, you can tell me everything. In the meantime, you have clothes here. Some are hanging in my bedroom closet, and some are in the top right drawer of my dresser. If you need the internet, the password is "Bruno1." There are also some business cards on my dresser if you need to call me."

"I don't have a phone," I said.

"I have a landline," she said. "There is a phone in the kitchen and another in the bedroom."

"A landline, huh?" I said.

"They do still exist, ya know," she said.

"I didn't say anything," I said with a smile.

"I have to go," she said as she attached Bruno's leash. She then took her car keys that were hanging on a key rack by the door. She pointed at the remaining key and said, "Here is a spare key in case you leave." She started out the door but came back and kissed me on the cheek. "I hope you are here when I get home."

I smiled as I watched her and Bruno walk out the door.

Chapter 14

I didn't like having the rental car parked nearby. Technically, the rental term wasn't up, so the rental company wouldn't be looking for it, but Parker could have possibly put pressure on them to find it. I didn't know if their cars were traceable by GPS, but I didn't want to take that chance. I decided that they would likely find the car soon, so I decided to return it. I got the rental receipt from the glove box and looked up the address. It was relatively close but not so close that it would give away my location if I returned it there. I took Annie's spare key and headed out the door.

When I got to the rental car place, I parked the car in their return lot, grabbed my jacket, and dropped the keys in the box. The office was open, but I saw no reason to go inside.

As I was driving to the rental car place, I noticed a mobile phone store about a block away. I walked there and purchased a cheap smartphone and a 2-gigabyte phone card. I thought phone cards were sold by the minute, but I had been out of it for a while. The woman there helped me set up the phone, and when I left, I called a cab to take me back to Annie's apartment.

Once back at the apartment, I poked through the kitchen for something to eat. I probably needed to eat healthier, and here was my chance. On the counter were apples, bananas, peaches, and tomatoes. She also had onions, garlic, sweet potatoes, and some kind of squash. In the refrigerator was a big tub of spring mix, yogurt, eggs, blueberries, and a half gallon of coconut milk.

I should have made a nice salad, but I felt a bit lazy. I checked the cabinet and found what I was looking for; cereal. It was granola but close enough. I poured some into a bowl, added blueberries and a little coconut milk, and brought it into the living room. I turned the television on and found a news channel. I thought there was a slight chance that Parker or Gabby might be on the news, but I saw nothing about them. I assumed it was just a local Florida story.

I finished the cereal, washed the bowl, and got the business card from Annie's dresser. I took out my burner phone and dialed the number on the card. Annie picked up on the second ring, "Officer Hansen."

"Annie," I said. "It's uh, John."

"John! Are you okay?" she said. "I thought you didn't have a phone."

"I bought it today," I said. "It's not traceable to me. I wanted you to have my number."

"That's good," she said. "Where are you now?"

"I'm back at your apartment," I said. "I hope you don't mind, but I ate some of your food."

"You wouldn't be John if you didn't," she said. "I'll be home in a few hours. If you plan on staying, I'll pick up a pizza on the way home."

"That sounds great," I said. "Judging by what is in your kitchen, I'm surprised you eat pizza."

"I know you love pizza, John. I love it too. I try to eat healthy, but sometimes cheating is good for the soul." She then added, "I'm only talking about food cheating."

"I figured as much. I look forward to eating pizza with you tonight," I said, feeling like a teenager on a first date. "Do you mind if I use your shower?"

"I would prefer that," she said. "I didn't want to say anything before, but I think a shower would benefit you greatly."

"I'm sorry," I said, embarrassed. "My resources have been limited lately."

"No worries. I understand."

I thanked her and hung up. I checked the dresser drawer and found several pairs of underwear and socks. In the closet were two T-shirts and a collared button-up shirt. There were also two pairs of pants, both tan. One looked like tactical pants with several pockets for holding stuff. The other looked like khakis. I pulled out the collared shirt and khakis. I figured I should look nice.

After I showered and dressed, I wanted to brush my teeth. I saw two toothbrushes in the bathroom. I assumed one was mine, but I didn't know which one, so I just put some toothpaste on my finger and ran it across my teeth.

I went back into the living room and took out the laptop. I inserted the memory card with Dad's program and copied it to the computer. I didn't think I would need a copy, but if anything happened to the thumb drive, I would still have something for leverage. I changed the name to random numbers and letters and stuck it in the Windows folder. I figured nobody would think to look there. I then copied the video of Parker and Rafferty to the memory card. After that, I copied it to my phone as well.

Next, I created an email account and wrote an email to Alex. I told him everything I learned since we last talked and gave him my new phone number in a way that only Alex would understand, just in case someone hacked his email. I signed it "John." I sent off the email and closed the computer. I needed to think. After a while and no real solutions, I decided to busy myself with something else.

I found the silverware and plates and set the table. I put out napkins and even found a couple of candles that I put on the table. I found a bottle of wine under the cabinet but hesitated to open it in case Annie didn't drink alcohol and just had it for guests. Instead, I put a couple of glasses on the table and filled them with ice and spring water from the fridge.

I lit the candles ten minutes later when I saw Annie's police cruiser pull in. The door opened, and Bruno came running in. I was standing in the dining room. When he saw me, his tail started wagging, and he ran up to me, put his paws on my chest, and started licking my face again, just like the first time he saw me. "Bruno, get down," Annie said. It was less of a command and more of a polite request, so Bruno ignored her. "Bruno! Sit!" she said more sternly. This time Bruno sat but continued wagging his tail.

I saw Annie standing by the door with a pizza box in her hand. "Oh, my," she said. "You set the table. How romantic."

"I know we are technically engaged to be married, but for me, this feels like a first date," I said.

"I'll be honest, John, I don't know how to feel right now," she said. "On the one hand, I feel like I need to mourn John's loss. On the other hand, I want to celebrate his return."

"It is certainly a difficult situation," I said. "I have been having more conflicting feelings lately than anyone should ever have. Just being with you is a conflict for me."

"You mentioned you have a wife as that other person," Annie said.

"Her name is Lisa," I said. "She is Alex's wife, not mine. I have come to accept that, but it is difficult. I know I just need to move on and live my own life."

"Well, for now, let us just enjoy this pizza," Annie said.

"I Agree'" I said, and I opened the box and put a couple of slices on each of our plates.

The pizza had peppers, onions, olives, and another vegetable that I couldn't identify but no meat. "Are you a vegetarian?" I asked. "I noticed there is no meat in your fridge."

"I don't like to label myself like that," she said. "I don't want to put myself in a box that dictates what I can and can't eat. If I want to eat meat, I will. I just usually prefer to avoid it."

"I never thought about it that way, but you are right. You are wise beyond your years," I said before taking another bite of pizza.

Annie had a look of surprise in her eyes. "You've told me that before," she said. "Are you sure John is not in there with you?"

"To be honest, I'm not so sure," I said. "I don't think I remember anything from John's life, but when I first saw you, there was a flash of familiarity. Also, how I feel seems different. I feel less intimidated by other people. I seem to have a confidence that I never had before."

"John was overflowing with confidence," she said. "I loved that about him."

"Well, I'm confident I could eat another slice of pizza," I said. "How about you?"

"Give me the big one," she said.

I assumed she was referring to the pizza, so I took out the biggest slice and put it on her plate. "The big one for the pretty lady," I said, smiling. I then found the next biggest slice and put it on my plate.

"Do you really think I'm pretty?" she asked.

"Of course. Who wouldn't?"

"What do you find pretty about me?" She asked. "What is most appealing to you?"

I looked at her for a moment and then said, "Your eyes. I love your deep blue eyes. They are like the beautiful blue waters of a tropical paradise."

She smiled and said, "What else?"

"What else?" I repeated. "What do you mean?"

"What else do you find attractive?" she said.

"Well, this is another example of how I have changed. If I had met you as Alex, I would have never been comfortable telling you how beautiful your breasts are. Even under that uniform, your figure looks fantastic."

"Now I know John is in there," she said as she leaned over to kiss me. I put my arms around her and kissed her back. It became uncontrollably passionate as Annie climbed on top of me. We kissed for another thirty seconds, and then she leaned back and slowly unbuttoned her blouse. She slipped her left arm out and then her right and returned to kissing me.

She was wearing a cream-colored lace bra that highlighted her ample breasts. Probably not police issue, I thought. She reached behind her back and unhooked the bra, then removed it and let it fall to the floor. She then grabbed my hands and placed them on her breasts. They felt soft and silky smooth. "How do you feel about them now?" she said.

"I've almost forgotten about your eyes," I said as I put my arms around her. I kissed her again, stood up, and carried her to the bedroom. We made love for what seemed like hours, then fell asleep in each other's arms.

Chapter 15

I awoke to a strange feeling. I opened my eyes and saw Bruno at the edge of the bed, pressing his nose against my feet. When he saw I was awake, his tail started wagging, and he let out a couple of loud whines.

"Bruno needs to go out," Annie said. I looked over at her. Her eyes were still closed, and her hair was a mess. She was a beautiful sight.

"I'll take him," I said. "Go back to sleep."

"Mmmm," was all I heard.

I dressed and found Bruno's leash hanging on a hook in the kitchen. Near it was a container holding plastic poop bags. I grabbed a couple of bags and attached his leash to his collar. I looked through the front window and saw an orange glow on the horizon. The sun had not yet come up. As I opened the door, Bruno's tail immediately started wagging faster. He pulled me out the door and headed to the nearest bush to relieve himself.

Once he was free of the burden of needing to pee, he was able to smell everything at his leisure. We walked along the side of the building while he smelled every bush and shrub along the way. We then walked toward the parking lot, where Bruno spent an equal amount of time smelling the fronts of all the cars along the sidewalk. He paid particular attention to a white Ford Explorer. He first smelled the front of the vehicle and then moved around to the front driver's side tire. After smelling every inch of the tire, he lifted his leg and peed on it. I looked around to see if anyone was looking. I saw a young couple outside but looking in another direction. "C'mon Bruno," I said as I pulled his leash. He got the hint, and we quickly walked away from the scene of the crime.

We came upon the young couple. Both looked to be in their early twenties. The woman had just finished hooking a baby into a car seat. "Good morning, John," the man said. "Long time no see. We were worried that you and Annie broke up."

"Oh, no," I said. "I was just away on business."

"I see," he said. "Well, it is good to see you again."

Thank you," I said. "It's good to be back."

With that, they both got in the car and drove away. I continued to walk Bruno for another ten or fifteen minutes, but he didn't need to poop, so I brought him home.

When I returned, I saw Annie standing in the kitchen making coffee. She was wearing panties and the button-up shirt she had on the previous night, except this time, she was wearing no bra and only had it buttoned halfway up. I put Bruno's leash away and gave her a long, passionate kiss while I reached around and grabbed her ass. She playfully pushed me away and said, "You are quite the horn toad. Didn't you get enough last night?"

"Today is a new day," I said.

"Yes, it is," she said. "That means we have plenty of time for that later. Do you want some coffee?"

"I'd love some," I said.

She proceeded to pour two cups of coffee and added a little cream to both cups. She put the cups on the table and motioned for me to sit down, which we both did.

"This is really good coffee," I said.

"Your memory may be screwed up, but your taste buds haven't been affected," she said.

"So, John was a coffee drinker too?" I asked.

"You are John. You need to remember who you are. This Alex fellow, he's not you."

"I have been thinking a lot about that lately," I said. "I need to have my own life. If I am John, I need to be John. Can you help me with that?"

"I thought you would never ask," she said. "We can start today. I have the day off. But first, we need to get ready. You're taking me out for breakfast."

We took a shower together. I washed her, and she washed me. Despite what she said earlier, we were soon going at it again. I don't know how much water we let go down the drain, and I didn't care. When we finished, we got dressed and headed out.

We took Bruno with us, and Annie led us to the white Ford Explorer. She opened the back door, and Bruno jumped inside. We then both climbed inside. "So, this is yours?" I asked rhetorically.

"Yes," she said. "Why?"

"Oh, uh, no reason," I said. "I guess I just assumed you drove your police vehicle."

"They let us bring our vehicle home, but when I am driving it, I feel like I am on duty, even when I am not," she said. "On my days off, I don't want that responsibility."

We drove about two miles to a strip mall. The end unit was a local family restaurant that served breakfast and lunch. The parking lot was almost full, but someone had just pulled out of one of the front parking spaces, and Annie pulled in. She put it in park and said, "We come here a lot. It's one of the few dog-friendly restaurants in the area.

The place had four tables on the front sidewalk. An elderly couple was sitting at the far-left table. Bruno took an interest in their Basset Hound lying under their table. Annie, sensing a potential problem, directed us to the far-right table. The other two tables were empty. It was still a bit cold outside, so it was probably not an ideal spot to have breakfast for anyone without a dog. The cold didn't bother me, which was surprising because I was born and raised in Florida. On the other hand, John was a Virginia-raised Army Ranger.

Our waiter came to our table with a bowl of water he had put down for Bruno. He looked a lot like Tony Soprano. "Good morning, Annie," he said. "Hello, John. Do you want the usual this morning?"

"Sure," Annie said.

"Me too," I said, not knowing what to expect, but I figured if John liked it, so would I.

"I think now is a good time to tell me everything," Annie said. "I especially want to know how you knew to look for me."

"It was a lucky coincidence that I ran into your brother at his hotel," I said. "He was not happy with me. He thought I got cold feet and walked out on you. I wanted to tell him the truth but couldn't think of a way to say it without making me look even worse. "

"The thought that you got cold feet did occur to me, too," she said.

"I would have been a fool to even think about doing that to you."

"That thought also occurred to me. You left the Army to be with me, John. You wouldn't give that up just to abandon me. That's why I thought you were dead."

Just then, our waiter came with our coffee. He put them on the table and said, "Your food should be out shortly."

"Thank you," we said in unison before he walked away.

I told Annie my story, starting with the day we met Dad in the lab. I reached the part where I met Gabriella when our food arrived.

Annie got an omelet with some kind of potatoes. I got bacon, sausage, and eggs, sunny side up with toast. I don't know why, but I was expecting what I got. I broke the yolks of my eggs and picked up a piece of toast, and dipped it in the juice. I looked up and saw Annie staring at me.

"What?" I asked.

"Nothing. It's just that you always do that thing with your eggs and toast."

"I do? That is weird. I don't remember ever doing that before."

Annie just smiled. I knew she was thinking that John was still in there, and I didn't have the heart to disappoint her. On the other hand, I couldn't deny that there were plenty of differences between the new me and the old me. I changed the subject and finished my story.

While I was talking, we ate our breakfast. I slipped a sausage and a piece of bacon to Bruno, who quickly gobbled them up. When I finished talking, she shook her head and said, "That's a terrible story. I'm so sorry about your father. Where do you think that woman is now?"

"Gabby? I'm sure she is looking for me. That's why I hesitate to stay with you too long. I don't want to put you in any danger."

"Don't worry about me," Annie said. "I'll kick her ass if I see her."

"I'd love to see that," I said, "but I don't want to sit around and wait for her. The best thing I can do right now is to get my life in order, and the best way to do that is to be John. That's why I need your help. Where do I live? Do you think we can go there next?

"Since you left the Army, you have been splitting your time between your parent's house and my apartment, but most of your stuff is at their house," she said. "We were planning on buying a house together after we got married."

"When is that?" I said.

"June 29th," she said. "We still have a place booked. I didn't cancel it."

"Don't cancel it," I blurted out, not knowing why. "I mean, I've only known you for a day, less than a day. Even so, I can't help feeling a strong connection to you. I don't know how we will feel about each other a week from now or a month, but I would like to find out."

Annie reached her hand out and put it on mine and just smiled.

Just then, the waiter came and asked if everything was okay. We told him the food was delicious and we were ready for the check. He reached into his pocket, found our check, and put it upside down on the table. I reached for it, but Annie grabbed it first. "I'll get this," she said. "I'm sure your money is limited right now."

"You've got that right," I said. "Thank you."

She put down enough cash to cover the check plus a tip and said, "Let's go. I think it's time to meet your parents."

Once we got on the road, Annie told me she had already planned to take me to see my parents today. She said she called them while I was outside walking Bruno. She told them I was alive. She also told them I was involved in some kind of an accident that caused me to lose my memory. I agreed that telling my parents the truth would have been too much for them. It's better that their son should lose his memories than to have them replaced by someone else's. It left them with the hope that the memories might return.

"You never told me how we met," I said.

"We grew up together," Annie said. "You lived down the street from me. We went to school together from kindergarten until after the fifth grade. That's when your parents bought a house outside of the school district. I didn't see you again until I gave you a ticket for speeding. It was almost three years ago. You had recently returned from Afghanistan at the time. That was when I was a rookie before I was in the canine division."

"You gave me a ticket even after knowing who I was?"

"You were speeding. Besides, it didn't stop you from asking me out."

"I'm surprised you were free," I said. "A girl as pretty as you should have men knocking down your door."

She smiled, embarrassed, and said, "You'd be surprised how many men are turned off by strong women."

"I don't know. I find it to be a turn-on."

"That is why we are together," she said.

We drove about twenty minutes and came upon a nice, suburban neighborhood. We passed several big houses with large, manicured yards. We pulled into the driveway of a beautiful, two-story home with a two-car garage attached to the side. Annie turned the engine off and said, "Are you ready for this?"

"No," I said. "Let's go."

Chapter 16

Annie got Bruno out of the back seat, and as the three of us approached the house. The front door opened and out came an attractive middle-aged woman with shoulder-length dark hair gently swaying as she walked across the porch. She wore a grey pantsuit and looked like she might be heading off to work. Behind her was a fit-looking, middle-aged man with sandy blond hair. I could see the resemblance in me. He was wearing dress pants and a dress shirt but no tie. When we got close enough, the woman threw her arms around me and said, "John, we are so happy to see you. Annie told us what happened." She pulled away and wiped the tears out of her eyes.

The man then hugged me and said, "Welcome home, son. We are so happy you are alive. We were naturally worried when you disappeared, but we never gave up hope."

"I'm sorry I can't remember," I said. "I wish I could. You both seem very nice. I bet I had a good childhood."

"I think you did," the woman said. "You were mostly a happy child."

"Mostly?"

"Well, everybody has off days."

"I hope we are not interrupting," I said. "You two seemed dressed up. Were you heading out?"

"Your parents own a construction company," Annie said. "They stayed home when I told them we were coming because they wanted to see you."

"Do you really not remember?" the man asked.

"I'm sorry. I don't remember anything," I said.

"Well, I'm Marie, and this is John Senior, but you can just call us Mom and Dad," she said.

"C'mon inside," Dad said, and we followed them into the house.

After we got inside, we walked to the right into a large living room. Annie and I sat on a sofa to the left. Bruno lay on the floor next to Annie. Mom and Dad sat on a loveseat to our left. Behind them, to the right, was a gun case tucked away in the corner with four rifles inside.

Dad saw me looking at it and said, "You used to go deer hunting every fall since you were fourteen. I would take you out of school for a week. Mom hated it, but I thought a week of real-world experience was better than anything you could learn in school. It didn't take long before you were shooting better than me. Do you remember any of that?"

"I'm sorry, Dad, I don't. Those sound like great memories."

"No need to be sorry, son. I'm sure it will come back to you in time."

"Perhaps we can do it again sometime," I said.

"I would love that," Dad said.

"Can I get you two anything?" Mom interrupted.

"No, thanks," I said. "We just had breakfast."

"Oh, too bad. I could have cooked something for you."

"I'd love to take a rain check on that."

"Of course," she said. "Do you want to look around? Maybe something will jog your memory."

"Sure," I said, and we all got up for a tour of the house.

Mom led the tour, with Dad following us. She showed us the kitchen, which was very large with an island in the middle. The back door was next to the kitchen. She took us outside to see the large deck they had recently built onto the house. The master bedroom was near the kitchen and had a sliding door that opened onto the deck.

Mom then took us upstairs to show us my bedroom. On the way up, I noticed many family photos hanging on the wall. One picture caught my eye. I was sure I had seen it before. It was a boy, perhaps thirteen years old, standing on a pier next to a girl, maybe eight years old. The girl was holding a fishing pole with a small fish hanging from it. She had a big smile like she was proud of herself for catching the fish.

"I've seen this photo before," I said. "I don't know how, but I remember this."

"Are you sure?" Annie said.

"Yes," I said. "How is this possible?"

"This is great news," Dad said. "It's a sign your memory is returning."

"That is a picture of you and your sister, Joanie," Mom said. "You were teaching her how to fish."

Suddenly a feeling of intense sadness came over me. "She died, didn't she?" I said.

Mom looked at Dad and back at me, "Yes, she did. That is the last photograph we have of her."

"I have a vague recollection of a car accident."

"We were coming back from a camping trip. The one where that photo was taken," Mom said as she wiped tears from her eyes. "A garbage truck ran a red light and slammed into our car where Joanie was sitting. You were sitting beside her and, thankfully, only had a few bruises. At that point, she started crying and turned her head so I wouldn't see her.

I put my hand on her shoulder and said, "It's okay to be sad, Mom."

She shook her head and wiped her eyes, "No, this is a happy day. Let's go check out your room."

We continued up the stairs, and Mom opened the bedroom door. I walked in first, followed by Mom, Annie, and Dad. A full-size bed was against the far wall under a window. To the left was a closet that took up the entire wall. To the right was a dresser, and next to the door was a four-drawer chest with a television on it. Nothing was hanging on the walls. "Do I keep it this clean?" I asked.

"You've been known to make a mess or two in your lifetime, but since you joined the Army, you've become a bit of a clean freak. I just wish you had joined when you were five." Mom said, and we all laughed.

"Would you mind giving us a few minutes?" I asked.

"C'mon, Marie," Dad said. "We'll be downstairs if you need us." They stepped out and closed the door behind them.

"You remembered something," Annie said. "I told you John was in there."

"Yes, and now I can't help but wonder if there are other memories of John's that I think belong to Alex."

"Only time will tell, but I suspect you have more than one of John's memories floating around in your head."

"Listen," I said. "My parents seem like good people. You were smart to tell them what you did. If we discover more memories that belong to John, we should probably tell them. I think they will be happy to know it, but I don't want them to have unrealistic expectations."

"We'll cross that bridge when we come to it. Let's just see what we can find that could be useful."

"A driver's license would be helpful," I said.

Annie looked through the chest, and I checked the dresser drawers. "We should pack some of your clothes. You can stay with me until we figure everything out."

"I can't think of anywhere I'd rather be."

The drawers contained nothing useful, so we checked the closet. Several jackets, shirts, pants, and John's Army uniform, hung on the right side of the closet. The left side was mostly empty except for a few hand weights and a couple of boxes of memorabilia from John's school days. On the shelf was a small safe, about the size of a toaster oven. I pulled it out and put it on the bed. It had an electronic keypad with numbers on it. "Do you know the combination?" I asked Annie.

"No, but there is a fingerprint scanner."

"I think our luck is improving," I said as I pressed my index finger against the scanner. Nothing happened.

"Try your left hand," Annie said.

I put my left index finger against the scanner, and it opened. Inside was a handgun and a holster. I said, "Am I left-handed?"

"No," Annie said. "Knowing you, you probably thought it was more efficient to use your left hand. That way, you could use your right hand to throw open the top and grab the gun.

"That makes sense," I said as I took the gun out to look at it. I didn't know anything about guns, but I thought it would be helpful to have it.

I set the gun on the bed along with its holster. I also found a passport in the safe. I looked at it and saw it was current. "It's not a driver's license, but it is helpful."

Under the passport was a money clip with ten one-hundred-dollar bills. I looked at Annie and asked, "Was I worried about something? This looks like the beginning of a go bag."

"If you were worried about something, you didn't tell me," she said. "It could be that you just wanted to be ready for anything."

"There's something else in here," I said. I pulled out a small box and opened it. Inside was a beautiful diamond engagement ring and a diamond-studded wedding band. I showed it to Annie.

"Oh my God," she said. "They're beautiful. You asked me to marry you about a month before you disappeared. You said you were saving for a ring, but I had no idea you bought it."

"Here, try it on," I said and put the ring on her finger.

She held her hand up to the light and said, "It's perfect. I love it. Thank you." She kissed me and then checked out her ring again.

"I wish I could take more credit for it. My parents are going to wonder about us. We should find a bag and pack up this stuff."

I found a gym bag in the closet and put some clothes in it along with the gun, money, passport, and wedding ring. Annie kept the engagement ring on her finger. We headed downstairs and found Mom, Dad, and Bruno waiting for us in the living room.

"You're taking clothes with you, son?" Dad said. "We thought maybe you would want to stay here for a while."

"I'd like that, Dad, but Annie is helping me put my life in order, and I need her right now. I hope you understand."

"I see you gave her the ring," Mom said.

"You knew about that?" I asked.

"Of course. You asked my help in picking it out."

"Well, he certainly went to the right person for advice," Annie said, looking at the ring again.

"He loves you more than you know," Mom said. "I don't know if this memory problem has affected your relationship but remember, love comes from the heart. Love doesn't forget."

"I'll remember that," Annie said.

"I hate to leave so quickly," I said, but we have a lot to do today. As soon as I get my affairs in order, I want to come back here and reminisce about my life with you."

"This is your home," Mom said. "You are always welcome."

"Thank you both so much," I said.

"Thank you," Annie said.

"Wait," Dad said. "Don't you want to see your car?"

"My car?" I said.

"Yes," he said. "You spent years restoring it."

We all went to the garage from the outside, and Dad entered a code that opened the door on the left side. As it opened, it revealed the front end of a classic Mustang. Once fully opened, I saw it was a '69 Mustang Mach 1 Fastback. It was one of my dream cars when I was younger. I mean, when Alex was younger. This one was black with a red stripe down the side. "It's beautiful," I said. "A '69, right?"

"Yup," Dad said.

"Does it have the 428?" I asked.

"You seem to know a lot for a guy with memory loss," Dad said. "Are you remembering this?"

"I don't know," I said. "Maybe I am." I couldn't tell him Alex was fascinated by Mustangs. "Did I bring this to work?"

"No, he said, "you drove your Dakota."

"Where's that?" I asked.

"It was in Parker's lot," he said. It was impounded when you disappeared. The police needed it for their investigation. I've been trying to get it back, and they kept telling me soon, but I'm still waiting. Maybe it would be easier for you to get it back now that you are okay."

"I wouldn't exactly say I'm okay, Dad," I said.

"You're here, aren't you?" he said. "That's okay in my book."

"Didn't anyone wonder why I disappeared without my car?"

"Sure," he said. "We heard plenty of speculation. Of course, Parker covered his ass by hinting that you were mentally unstable. Naturally, I knew that was bullshit. Anyway, do you want to take the car for a drive?"

"I'd love to."

"The keys are in the ashtray. Go ahead."

I motioned to Annie to come with me, and we got in the car. It was almost perfect inside. It had black vinyl seats and a black dashboard. I retrieved the key from the ashtray, put it in the ignition, then started the engine. It came to life with a roar. I pulled it out of the garage slowly and then turned right onto the street.

"I know a good road," Annie said, directing me out of the neighborhood. After about five minutes, we were in a rural area on a straight and flat stretch of road.

"Let's see what this baby's got," I said and pushed down on the accelerator. Immediately we were pressed into our seats as the car quickly exceeded 100 miles per hour. The speed felt exhilarating, but I was not used to driving that fast, so it also made me a bit nervous. I decided to slow down and turn around. I figured one more time wouldn't hurt, so I pushed it past 110 this time before slowing down and heading back.

When we got back to the house, I backed the car into the garage, closed the door, and we went inside to say our goodbyes. We all hugged again before collecting Bruno and heading out. We got in Annie's Explorer and backed out of the driveway as Mom and Dad waved.

"Did you enjoy your visit?" Annie said.

"I did," I said. "My parents are nice people. I wanted to stay longer, but I don't feel comfortable sitting around doing nothing while Parker and Gabriella are out looking for me. I want to prepare for them."

"Do you have a plan?" she said.

"No, but I have been pretty good at winging it so far," I said.

"So, winging it is your plan?" she asked.

"I'm open to suggestions."

She didn't reply. We both just looked out the window for a while, and then I said, "Can you teach me how to use a gun?"

"You don't know?" she said.

"I never needed a gun before," I said.

"Alex never needed a gun," she said. "You most certainly did. Firing a gun is something that should be engraved in your soul. Your mind may not know, but your body surely does."

"My body may know, but my mind doesn't," I said. "Please help me get the two into sync."

 Okay," she said. "I know a place we can go."

Chapter 17

We drove back to Annie's place, where we took Bruno for a walk. When we were done, Annie said, "I'll be right back," and went inside the apartment with Bruno.

I waited outside for a couple of minutes until Annie returned holding two bags. She handed one to me and said, "Here you go."

"What's this?"

"It's your range bag. You keep it at my place."

I unzipped it and saw a pair of safety goggles, earmuffs, bullets, and a couple of other things I didn't recognize. "Did we go shooting together a lot?" I asked.

Our schedules didn't always mesh, but we would hit the range two or three times a month," she said.

I moved my gun to my range bag and put both bags in the back seat. Once on the road, I said, "You told me I left the Army to be with you. What do I do for a living now?"

"You work for a private security company," she said. "Not too long ago, they got a contract to work for Parker Biosystems, protecting their main research lab. They were developing something that needed protecting, as you are aware."

"So, I didn't work directly for Parker?" I asked.

"Hell no," she said. "You thought Parker was a jackass."

"Interesting," I said.

The shooting range was about ten minutes from Annie's apartment. We pulled into the parking lot while I was still thinking about what Annie told me. We went inside, checked in, and bought a couple of dozen targets. Before going inside, we put on our safety glasses and earmuffs. This section of the range had six stations. A man stood at the far station loading his weapon while talking to a woman beside him. They were probably a couple. Annie put her bag on the bench at the second station and directed me to the first. She pulled out my gun, unloaded it, and put it on the bench.

"There are some rules you need to know," she said loudly so I could hear with the earmuffs on. "First, treat every gun as if it is loaded. Second, always point your weapon downrange. Third, never set a loaded gun on the counter. Always remove the cartridge and clear the chamber like you just saw me do. Fourth, never put your finger on the trigger until you are ready to fire. Fifth, listen for any ceasefire order and obey. Sixth, always be aware of your surroundings. That means knowing where people are around you. Do you understand all of that?"

"Yes," I said.

"Good," she said. She picked up the magazine and removed the bullets. "Now, to load the magazine, you want to hold it with your left hand with your thumb on top like this, then push the bullets down and in."

She put all the bullets back in, took them out again, and handed me the magazine. "Here, try it. The first one is easy, but the rest take some getting used to."

I put the magazine in my left hand like she showed me and put the bullets in until it was fully loaded. "There," I said. "That wasn't so hard."

"Very good," she said. "You have a speed loader in your bag, but there is no need to show you that right now. You obviously don't need it. Now, pick up the gun but don't load it yet. Show me how you would hold it to fire."

I picked up the gun. It felt good in my hands. I found a comfortable position and aimed. There was no target yet, so I just imagined Gabby standing there, pointing a gun back at me. Annie checked me over and said, "You are a natural at this."

Next, she attached one of the targets. This one had the form of a human torso. She sent it back about ten yards and said, "Let's see what you got."

I picked up the gun, put the magazine in, set up my shot, and fired five rounds. I then removed the magazine and the bullet in the chamber and set the gun on the counter.

I looked at Annie and said, "What do you think?"

She pulled the target in and removed it. Two of the shots hit the center oval, two were inside the next oval, and one shot was inside the third oval. "This is good," she said. "I told you it was muscle memory, but you are capable of even better. I've seen it. So, let's keep going until you can get seven out of ten inside the bullseye."

Annie took out her weapon and practiced alongside me. We each shot ten times before replacing the target. It felt like a contest, although neither of us said anything about it. Annie came close to reaching the seven shots a couple of times. After about the tenth attempt, I pulled in a target that had seven bullseyes and one that was on the line.

"It is time for us to leave, Grasshopper," Annie said.

I caught the Kung Fu reference, bowed, and said, "Thank you, Master Annie."

We packed our stuff, cleaned up what we could, and headed out. As we were driving out of the parking lot, my burner phone started ringing. Annie looked at me, and I looked at the phone. It was a 727 number. "It must be Alex," I said.

I hit the answer button and put it on speaker. "Hello. Alex?"

"They took her!" he said. "They took Lisa!"

Chapter 18

"Wait a minute," I said. "What did you say?"

"We did what you told us to do," he said. "We got out of town. We went camping. That monster of a woman showed up with two henchmen very early this morning. They took Lisa. She said if she didn't get her thumb drive, they would kill her. I told her I didn't know where you were. She said she would give me more instructions tomorrow, and if I couldn't find you, it would be too bad for Lisa. Luckily I remembered to check my Yahoo email."

"Shit!" I said. "Did you call the police?"

"No! She said Lisa would die if I did that," he said.

"Don't worry," I said. "They need her alive. Call me as soon as you hear back from her."

"I will," he said. "I don't have to tell you how much she means to me."

"I know," I said. "I will do everything in my power to keep her safe."

I hung up. Annie looked at me in shock. "The shit just hit the fan," I said.

"You should call the FBI," she said. "They have experience with kidnappings, and we can't do much from here."

"I'm sure Parker has connections in the FBI and many other government agencies." I said, "Do you think they could have found them at a campground with no communication devices on them without government assistance? Besides, they are coming here. They know I'm here. Maybe they don't know exactly where I am, but I'm sure they've learned I returned the rental car by now. She also gave Alex until tomorrow. That's probably because they will spend today driving Lisa up here."

"What do you want to do?" Annie asked.

"I don't know, but I'm getting hungry," I said. "Let's get a bite to eat, and we can talk about it."

"I know a nice Italian place," she said.

After a few minutes, we pulled into a shopping center. It was shaped like an L, with a supermarket on the left and many smaller stores taking up the rest of the space. The Italian restaurant was between a cell phone store and a nail salon. It had a vinyl cutout of a fork with noodles hanging from it on the window. It had a name like "Pasta Luigi's" or something like that.

It was a small place with only a few tables, but we managed to get the only table by the window. The waitress came over, handed us menus, and said, "Welcome. Can I get you something to drink?" She was an older lady, perhaps sixty, with an Italian accent.

"I'll have the Pinot Grigio," Annie said.

I knew nothing about wine, so I just said, "I'll have the same and some water, please."

"Okay," she said. "I'll give you a couple of minutes to look over the menu."

When she left, I said, "I told Alex not to worry, but the truth is I don't know what to do. These people are killers. If I give them the drive, they will probably kill her anyway. The fact that I have what they want is why she is still alive. Hell, it's probably why I'm still alive."

Annie put her hand on mine and said, "If you were confident that they wouldn't hurt her if you gave them the drive, would you do it, knowing what they could use it for?"

"If you are asking if I would risk handing over control of this country to a cold-blooded narcissist in exchange for Lisa's life, I would say yes," I said. "I know that I am being influenced by emotion, but I also think it is like

117

trading a certain bad thing for an uncertain worse thing. If we can save Lisa, there will still be a chance that we can stop Parker, too."

"So, we just need to figure out how to make the exchange in a way that would guarantee her life, like the old spy movies where they would exchange prisoners by walking them across a bridge," Annie said.

"That wouldn't work in this case because they would need to confirm the drive is legit before releasing Lisa. That means they would need Lisa and the thumb drive simultaneously. Once they confirm they have what they want, they will have no incentive to release her. Worse, they will have every incentive to kill her."

The server came back with our drinks, and I realized I hadn't looked at the menu, so I opened it and quickly scanned through it.

"Did you decide, or should I give you more time?" she said.

"I know what I want," Annie said. "What about you, John?"

"Go ahead and order," I said. I figured if we let her go, it would be ages before we saw her again, and I was hungry.

"I'll have the eggplant parmigiana with the house salad," Annie said.

"I think I will try the puttanesca with pasta fagioli," I said.

"Those are both excellent choices," she said before taking our menus and walking away.

"Do you think if I ordered hot water and ketchup, she would say that was an excellent choice?" I asked.

"Well, that would depend on what brand of ketchup you ordered," Annie said, and we both had a good laugh for a change.

"Back to more serious matters," Annie said. "I've accumulated some personal days. I'm going to take a couple of days off until this matter is settled."

"I appreciate that," I said, "but if something happened to you, I couldn't live with myself. I welcome your ideas, but I need to do this alone."

"Don't be chauvinistic. I'm not a damsel in distress. I can take care of myself."

"I'm sure you can, but you are mortal like everyone else."

"So are you. Don't you think I would feel the same way if I let something happen to you?"

I hadn't thought of it that way. "I'm sorry," I said. "I should have considered your feelings. Okay, we will work this as a team, but we will take no unnecessary risks."

"Agreed," Annie said.

"I have a few ideas. Nothing resembling a plan, yet, but a start," I said.

"Okay, Let's hear 'em."

"First, we need to control where the exchange is made," I said. "They will resist it. They will want us to think they are holding all the cards, but we have a couple of aces in our hand. I will need your help coming up with a place."

We bounced a few ideas back and forth until our food arrived. We decided to put our planning off to enjoy our dinner. We talked about food, our likes and dislikes. I mentioned that I didn't know what I liked anymore. We talked about family. I learned that Annie had an older sister who married an oil worker and moved to Alaska. I also learned that her parents divorced two years ago and sold the home she grew up in. They both still lived nearby and got along well, but she had no place she considered home anymore.

We finished our dinner, paid the bill, and headed back to Annie's apartment. Bruno was very happy to see us. Once Bruno settled down, Annie and I kissed, then kissed some more. I started to remove her shirt, but she stopped me and said, "Not now. Bruno needs a walk. Can you take him out? I'll take a shower while you're gone."

"I was hoping to shower with you," I said.

"The last time we did that, there wasn't much showering going on," she said.

"The best kind of shower.

"Just go, and don't dilly dally. I'll be waiting for you."

I took Bruno out for his walk. The sun had gone down, and the last hint of twilight was on the horizon, but the apartment complex was well-lit. Bruno made sure he marked a few bushes and then pooped. I picked it up and dropped the bag inside one of the pet waste receptacles that were scattered around the property. I didn't want to spend too much time away from Annie, not then, so I brought Bruno back inside.

When I got back inside, I put down some food for Bruno and walked into the bedroom. Annie had a towel wrapped around herself and brushed her hair while sitting in a chair at a small dressing table. "The shower is free," she said without looking back. "Don't make me wait too long. "

That was a challenge that I happily accepted. I showered quickly, dried up, brushed my teeth, and found Annie in bed under the covers with the light off. I turned the light on and said, "Sorry, but I want to see you."

I pulled the covers down, and this incredible feeling of good fortune came over me. I knew tomorrow would be different. Tomorrow could be my last day on Earth, but that night there was just her and me, and I intended to make the most of it.

Chapter 19

I woke up to my phone ringing. I looked at the clock. It was 7:03 a.m. I checked the number. It was Alex. I sat up in bed and hit the answer button. Annie, with concern on her face, sat up next to me. "Hello, Alex," I said.

"She called me this morning," he said. "She wants to meet you tonight at 7 p.m. She texted me the address. I'm forwarding it to you now. She said if you give her the memory card, she will give you Lisa. Do you believe her?"

"Not for a second," I said, "but don't worry, we will figure something out."

"Who's we?" he said.

"It's a long story. I'll tell you later," I said.

"I'm coming there to help," he said.

"And you're doing what with your kids?" I asked. "You need to stay there and take care of them. Don't forget, right now, you can be in two places at once, and the other you is a former Army Ranger."

"Please, just get her back," he said.

"I won't let you down," I said. "Let me know if she contacts you again, and I will keep you posted," I hung up the phone.

Annie put her hand in mine and said, "Where does she want to meet?"

I checked my text messages and showed her the address.

"There are mostly warehouses in that area," she said. "Give me a minute."

She got out her phone and typed in the address. After three or four minutes of searching, she finally said, "That is a warehouse building owned by Parker."

"We would be like sheep walking into a lion's den," I said. "We can't meet there."

"What if they insist?" Annie asked.

"There is no way in hell they will let Lisa go if I hand over the memory card," I said. "She is a witness. They can't have that."

"You are a witness, too."

"Not a credible one."

"What about the video you showed me?"

"That video makes them look bad, but it's not damning," I said. "Even so, I'm sure they wouldn't want it to go public, so we may have a use for it, but only if we can get them onto neutral ground. Have you thought about a good location?"

"I think I know a good place," she said, pulling out her phone and showing it to me on the map.

"The interstate?" I said.

"It's public. They won't dare shoot anybody there, but it is also anonymous enough that they would probably be okay with it.

"Good thinking," I said, and I picked up the phone to call Alex.

"Do you have another phone?" I said.

"I have Lisa's phone," he said. "They didn't take it."

"Good," I said. "Call the number that Gabriella used. Put both phones on speaker and hang up when I hang up. You won't want to but trust me."

"I hope you know what you are doing," he said and dialed the number.

Gabby answered and said, "Are you confirming the meeting?

"No," I said.

"It's the other Alex," she said.

"It's John now."

"Oh, you're going by the name I gave you, huh?" she said.

I had forgotten about the ID for John Miller that she gave me. "I'm going by the name that suits me," I said. "By the way, how's that bump on your head? I hope it doesn't leave a scar."

"Listen, John!" she said sternly. "If you ever want to see Lisa again, you will meet us when and where I say. Is that understood?"

"I understand that I have what you need for your evil plans. Without it, you will always be the nothing that you are today," I said. "I'm also not an idiot. Once you get the memory card, you will kill everyone so you can tie up all your little loose ends. I propose a new meeting place and time." I then told her exactly where I would be and said I would be there at 3 p.m. and wait no more than ten minutes."

"Absolutely not," Gabby said. "We are sticking to the original plan, or you can say goodbye to Lisa."

"Talk it over with your boss," I said, knowing that would irritate her. "If you want the thumb drive, that's where I'll be." I then hung up.

"That's a risky move," Annie said and put her hand on my face and kissed me. "Now it's time for Bruno's walk. Can you do that for me? Pleeeeese."

"How could I refuse a request like that?" I said before getting dressed to take Bruno for his walk.

When I returned, Annie was getting dressed. I brushed my teeth and finished getting ready. When both of us were dressed, Annie said, "Do you have a plan?"

"Less of a plan and more of an idea," I said. "For this, we will need to go back to my parents' house, and then we will need a police officer."

"I think I can help with both parts."

"I thought as much."

We got Bruno and headed to my parents' house. When we got there, I knocked on the door. Dad answered and said, "John, we didn't think we would see you again so soon."

"I'm sorry, Dad," I said. "We aren't here to visit. I need the car. It's very important."

Just then, Mom came to the door, "John, you shouldn't have to knock. Give him the spare key, dear."

Dad reached over, pulled a key off a holder near the door, and handed it to me. "Here you go," he said. "The garage door code is one less than our house number. The alarm code is the same."

"Thanks a lot, Dad. Thank you, Mom," I said and headed to the garage. I opened the door as Annie headed back to her vehicle. I pulled the Mustang out of the garage and saw Dad standing there. He closed the door behind me, and we waved at each other as I drove away.

We headed back to Annie's apartment. On the way, I called her and told her I was a little low on gas, so we stopped at a gas station near her apartment. I filled the tank with premium. I didn't think it would matter much, but I figured I could use every slight advantage I could get.

When we returned, the sprinklers in front of Annie's apartment were on. I found a small area of wet dirt, picked some up, and rubbed it on my license plate. It wasn't perfect, but it made the plate hard to read.

"What are you doing?" Annie said.

"I don't want them reading the license plate," I said. "It will lead them to my parents and possibly you."

"Pretty smart," she said.

After we went inside, I washed my hands, and Annie cooked us a couple of veggie omelets. It was 11:30 by then, too late for breakfast, but I didn't care. I was hungry, and they were good. She added a little cheddar cheese to them, which made them quite tasty.

After we ate, we made love again. We didn't talk about it, but I think we both knew we were embarking on something potentially deadly. I figured if today was my last day, I was going to make it a good one.

We stayed in bed until it was almost time to go, then we got dressed. I put my clothes back on, but Annie put on her police uniform. She put Bruno's police vest on while I attached my gun holster. It was a little awkward at first, but I soon found a comfortable position for it.

We left together and headed for the rendezvous point. I followed Annie to a fast-food restaurant near the onramp to the highway. She parked in their parking lot, and I pulled in next to her, got out, and went to her door. She lowered the window and kissed me.

"If this goes sideways," I said, "I want you to know that even though it has only been a couple of days, I think, I mean, I know, well . . ."

"I love you too," she said. "Now, do what we planned, and we will be fine."

"Okay," I said and got back in my car. I pulled out of the parking lot and got onto the onramp. Once I merged onto the highway, I drove two-tenths of a mile, pulled over onto the shoulder, and waited. It was four minutes before three.

I waited until almost five minutes after three, and a car pulled in behind me. It was a white, four-door sedan. A man was driving, and Gabby was in the passenger seat. I picked up the phone and called Annie. "They're here," I said.

I saw the front doors open, so I got out of the car. Gabby and the driver came together in front of their vehicle. Her henchman pulled out his gun and pointed it at me, but he kept it low, probably to shield it from the view of oncoming traffic. Gabby was carrying a laptop in her right hand. "Do you have my thumb drive?"

"I want to see Lisa."

Gabby turned and nodded at the car. The passenger side back door opened, and Lisa came out. The other man in the car came out behind her. It was David, Gabby's so-called brother. He had a gun pressed to Lisa's back. The two of them moved alongside Gabby, who said, "That's far enough."

"Good to see you again, David," I said. I looked at Gabby and then back at him. "I assume you are not really her brother."

"Good deduction, Einstein," he said. "I'm not even Mexican. I'm Puerto Rican. We knew you couldn't tell a Puerto Rican from a Mexican if your life depended on it, and it kind of did."

I took the thumb drive out of my pocket and held it up. "This is what you want," I said. "Let her go, and I will give it to you."

Gabby looked at David, who grabbed Lisa's hair and pulled it down hard. She screamed. "Give it to me now," she said. "If it is legit, I will be happy to get rid of her."

I tossed the card to her, and she caught it with her left hand. She opened her laptop and inserted the thumb drive. She moved her finger around the touch sensor, hit a few keys, and stared at it intently for about thirty seconds. "I also included a video that may interest you," I said. "I have that scheduled to publish on several different video platforms by morning if I don't stop it."

Gabby watched the video and said, "This is nothing. Nobody will believe it is real. Even if they do, it's vague and proves nothing."

"Enough people will believe it to cause a cloud of doubt about what you are doing," I said. "There will have to be an investigation. I'm sure you don't want that."

"We got what we need," Gabby said, turning to David. "Take her back to the car."

Just then, Annie pulled behind their car with her lights flashing. The two men immediately tucked their guns in their pants. Annie got out, opened the back door, and let Bruno out. She approached and said, "Is everything okay here?"

"Yes, Officer," I said. "We had some car trouble, but these fine folks helped us figure out the problem. Come on, Lisa. We should get on the road."

I held my hand out, and she hesitated for a second but then walked toward me. David started to move, but Bruno growled at him and showed his teeth. He stopped.

Lisa and I got in the car, and just as I started to pull away, I saw more flashing lights. It was a state trooper. "Shit," I said.

"What's wrong?" Lisa asked.

"We just lost our protection."

Lisa looked through the mirror, probably trying to figure out what I was talking about, then looked at me. "What protection? Who exactly are you, anyway? First, you bring that psycho bitch into our lives, and then you rescue me from her."

I saw in the mirror that Gabby's car was back on the road, but the state trooper was still delaying Annie. "It would take too long to explain right now," I said and stepped on the gas. Suddenly the traffic started getting heavy. I saw Gabby's car gaining on us, so I jumped onto the shoulder and passed about ten cars before the exit came up. I quickly got into the exit lane, but that was also backed up. "Put your seatbelt on," I said, and we both buckled up.

Gabby's car was in the breakdown lane when I looked up. They were gaining on us, and we were stuck. The exit lane was long and narrow. There wasn't enough room to get on the shoulder and pass cars. Gabby's car had reached the exit, and only one car stood between us and them.

When we got to the end, I merged onto another busy road. The road had three lanes in each direction, and I managed to gain a little breathing room by weaving in and out of traffic, but the driver of the sedan was no slouch and soon picked up the lost ground.

I wanted to get out of the heavy traffic, so I jumped into the right lane and turned down a side street that looked good. It was between two shopping plazas. Once I cleared them, I was on a narrow, winding road. It was a risky move. I had no idea where the road led. It could have dead-ended ahead. We passed by several large homes, slowly gaining altitude. This place was hillier than the surrounding area.

I saw in the mirror that Gabby's car was keeping up with us, so I stepped on the gas. The road was winding and narrow. I was concerned that we would collide with another vehicle coming from the other direction, but my more immediate concern was behind us. I had a plan, but I needed to put some distance between us and them. I stepped on the gas hard and told Lisa to hang on. I was looking for a place to hide and soon found it.

The road ahead veered to the left and went down, but straight ahead was a driveway that went up a steep angle. I took the driveway at full speed and let gravity slow us down. When we reached the top, the driveway turned to the right, out of sight of the road.

I quickly got out of the car, pulled my gun, and pointed it over the trunk toward the turn of the driveway. I heard the car go by and relaxed. Just then, I heard the cocking sound of a shotgun. "Don't move," a voice said. "Put the gun down and turn around."

I set the gun on the car's trunk and slowly turned around. I kept my elbows down but put my hands up so he could see they were empty. "I can explain," I said.

"You're on my property, uninvited," he said. He was an older man with white hair and a white beard.

"Yes, I'm sorry about that," I said. "People are trying to kill us. We used your property to escape them."

"Right," the man said. "Who are you really, and why are you on my property?"

By then, Lisa was out of the car and said, "He's telling you the truth. I was kidnapped, and this man saved my life."

The man looked at me, and I said, "Well, it didn't go exactly as planned. That is why I was pointing my gun at the driveway. People were pursuing us."

"That sounds like a bullshit story to me," the man said.

Just then, my phone rang. "Can I get this?" I asked the man with the gun.

"Slowly," he said.

It was Annie. I answered and said, "Hi Annie, we're okay," and then added, "for the moment. We have a situation here. In our attempt to save ourselves, we ended up trespassing and are now being held at gunpoint by a man who is not happy that we drove onto his property. I'm going to put you on speaker. Can you tell him the truth about what just happened?"

I pushed the speaker button and held the phone out. Annie said, "Sir, my name is Annie Hansen. I am a police officer with the Fredericksburg Police Department. About twenty minutes ago, I aided in a kidnapping rescue attempt. Unforeseen circumstances caused me to fail in my duty to protect the two with you now. I would greatly appreciate it if you could put your gun down and give me your address so I can come and help these people get to safety."

The man thought about it for a few seconds and said, "Send a photo of your badge first."

"Fine," Annie said. "Give me a minute."

After about a minute, the phone beeped. I opened the message and handed the phone to the man. He looked at the photo and then lowered his shotgun. "It looks like you two were telling the truth. I'm glad you both are okay, and I'm sorry for pointing a gun at you. A person just can't be too careful, if you know what I mean."

"I totally understand," I said.

He told Annie his address and handed the phone back to me. "You two are welcome to stay here until the officer arrives," he said.

"Thank you so much," I said.

I took the phone off speaker, put it to my ear, and said, "Thanks, Annie. Everything is good now. We'll wait here for you."

"Do you think you can stay out of trouble until I get there?"

"That's a big ask. See you soon."

"Would you folks like some coffee or something?" the man asked.

"That is very nice of you," I said, "but coffee and excitement don't mix very well. I think we will just wait here until my friend arrives."

"The police officer is your friend?" he asked.

"She is my fiancée," I said.

Lisa gave me a look of surprise, and the man said, "Well, congratulations. Do you two make a habit out of rescuing people?"

"This was the first one," I said, "but it was so much fun I'm thinking of starting a rescue business."

"The man laughed and said, "I'll leave you two alone now. If you need anything, just knock." He then turned and walked into the house.

Lisa looked at me and said, "Now you have time to tell me. What is going on here? You show up at our door with that woman who killed Alex's father and kidnapped me, and then you risk your life to rescue me. Now I hear you are engaged to a different woman. Does she know you were with that other woman?"

"It is a very long story," I said. "I want to tell you everything, but you wouldn't believe it. Plus, if you did believe it, things would get awkward for everyone."

"What the hell does that mean?" she asked.

"You should call your husband," I said, handing her my phone.

Lisa looked at me for a couple of seconds, dialed the number, and put the phone to her ear. "Hi honey, it's me. I'm fine. Yes. You're coming here? When? Do you have the kids? Okay, I'll tell him. I love you too. Bye."

She handed me back the phone and said, "He's on his way here with the kids. He said he will be here around nine. He wants you to text him the address."

"I told him not to come," I said.

"What would you do?"

"I guess I would have done the same thing."

I put Annie's address into a text message and sent it to Alex. I then looked up and saw Annie pull up in her police vehicle. She got out, walked over to me, and hugged me. She then put her hand out to Lisa and said, "Hi, I'm Annie."

They shook hands, and she said, "Nice to meet you. I'm Lisa."

"I'm so glad you two are okay," Annie said. "When that trooper showed up, I thought I lost you."

"Why are the police not involved in this?" Lisa said. "I mean, other than you. Why didn't you just tell that trooper what was going on?"

"It's complicated," I said. "Parker is wealthy and powerful. We don't know who is in his pocket. I'm sure that trooper was a good guy. I'm sure most are very honest. It's just that something like this is sure to go up the chain of command, and if just one link in that chain is bad, things could go very bad for us."

"What are we going to do now?" Lisa said.

We are going to wait for your husband to come and pick you up," I said. I looked at Annie and added, "He's on his way."

"We can wait at my place. You can ride back with me," Annie said as she opened the passenger door. "I want to hear everything about your husband, Alex." She walked around to the driver's side and winked at me as she opened her door and got in.

Chapter 20

When we returned to Annie's apartment, she handed me Bruno's leash and asked me to walk him. "Sure thing, my dear," I said. I wanted to remain pleasant, but I felt that Annie was trying to keep me away from Lisa. Was she jealous? I guess it would be understandable. I was, in a way, married to her. I knew what she looked like naked, and Annie knew that. She knew I had feelings for her even though I had mentally given her up.

When Bruno finished his business, we went inside and found Annie and Lisa at the dining room table. Annie was at the end of the table near the kitchen, and Lisa was sitting beside her on her left. Each had a cup of coffee in front of them. There was another cup on the table to Annie's right. "I poured you a cup, too," she said. "Have a seat."

I sat down next to Annie and took a sip from the cup. "Did you guys have a nice conversation on the way back?" I asked.

"We sure did," Annie said. "Lisa told me so much about her husband, Alex. She said he was a big nerd when she met him in college." She smiled at me when she said that.

"Is that so?" I asked. "What is he like now?"

"Still a nerd," Lisa said. "Maybe a little less nerdy, but I wouldn't have him any other way."

"I'm glad you two are happy," I said.

"I ordered Chinese food, by the way," Annie said.

"Good," I said. "I'm starving."

"Tell me," Lisa said, looking at me. "How are you involved in all this? You were quite vague earlier. What are you not telling me?"

"It's more complicated than you can imagine," I said.

"After the last few days, I can imagine a lot," she said. "Does Alex know? I will find out one way or another. Alex's father was killed. I was kidnapped. My family is in danger. I won't let this go."

"Can you give us a couple of minutes?" I asked and motioned for Annie to follow me.

We stepped outside and closed the door. I said, "I know this whole situation is difficult for you. Having the woman I remember being married to right here in your kitchen must be very hard. I can't tell you that I don't love her, but I can tell you that because I love her, I can let her go. She needs to be with the real Alex, and that is what I want for her. I have mentally let her go."

"Is that true? Do you really feel that way?" she asked.

"Yes, I do," I said. "I can tell you something else that's true. Even though my memory of you started only a couple of days ago, I feel like I've known you my whole life. I don't know how it happened so quickly, but I have fallen in love with you. I know I asked you before, Annie, but I'm asking again. Will you marry me?"

Annie wiped the tears from her eyes and kissed me. She hugged me and whispered in my ear, "I will."

When we finished hugging, I said, "Now, what should we tell her?"

"I think she deserves the truth," Annie said.

"I suppose she does."

With that out of the way, we went back inside and sat down with Lisa. I started by saying, "Lisa, do you remember when you went with Alex to see his father, and he ended up hooking you two up to his machine?"

"Did Alex tell you that?" she asked.

"Not exactly. Do you remember what the machine was designed to do?"

"Sure, it mapped all our memories or something like that."

"Do you know why Alex's dad then took a job with Parker Biosystems?" I asked.

"Not exactly. I think he wanted to find a way to give people their memories back."

"That's exactly right. They were working on a device that could take those recorded memories and reimplant them. Alex's dad learned Parker wanted to use the machine for something nefarious. The machine worked, but his father erased all the data pertaining to the recording of new memories. The only memories Parker had available were memories that were recorded years earlier. Those included Alex's memories."

She looked at me for several seconds and said, "What are you getting at?"

I looked over at Annie, who shrugged. I looked back at Lisa and said, "I was part of a security team assigned to protect the research project that was going on at Parker Biosystems. One day I overheard something I shouldn't have. To keep me quiet, they overwrote my memories with someone else's memories. That someone was Alex."

It took Lisa a little time to process what she heard. She looked at Annie, who nodded. She looked back at me and asked, "Are you saying you have Alex's memories?"

"That's exactly what I am saying," I said.

"I'm sorry, but that is just too crazy to believe," Lisa said.

"Ask me anything."

"Okay. Why did we pick our kids' names."

"You need to ask me something from before that day in the lab," I said. "However, I think I know the answer. Steven was your grandfather. He was killed in Vietnam when your mom was too young to remember him. His wife, Elizabeth, treated you very well, and you always talked fondly of her. She was still alive the last I remember."

"She passed away not long after that day in the lab."

"I'm so sorry," I said.

"Okay," Lisa said. "The night before we went to see your father at his lab, what did I tell you?

"You told me you were pregnant after you put Chinese take-out on our fancy dinnerware."

"I tried to make it special."

"You did make it special," I said. "Alex is lucky to have you. If you heard the same story from him, would you believe it?

"Yes," she said.

"Then call him," I said and handed her my phone.

She hesitated momentarily, then got up and said, "Okay, but I would like to talk privately." She dialed the number and stepped out the front door.

I looked at Annie and asked, "Do you think that was a mistake?"

"I guess we'll find out."

A couple of minutes later, the door opened, and Lisa came back inside. She handed me the phone and said, "Okay, I believe you, but I find this very weird. I don't know how I feel about a stranger knowing all my secrets. I mean, how do you even feel about me? I don't even know you. I can't have you obsessing over me. I love my husband."

"I know you love your husband, and he loves you. You have nothing to worry about, Lisa. I do love you as Alex does, but unlike Alex, I am not in love with you. I have come to terms with who I am. I may have Alex's memories, but I have John's body and his heart. I am in love with Annie. I reached over and squeezed Annie's hand. She squeezed back.

"That's a relief," she said. "I'm very happy for both of you. My concern now is what we are going to do. I mean, psycho bitch is still out there. What's to keep her from kidnapping me again, or worse, killing us?"

"Those are good questions," Annie said, "and to be honest, we don't know."

"We're working on it," I added. "I think you will be safe here until tomorrow."

"No," she said. "We can't stay here. Not knowing what I know now."

"You can't stay at a hotel," I said. "Once you run your credit card, they will know where you are."

"I'm sure they will take cash," Lisa said.

"Yes, but they still run your card and block off a few hundred dollars in case you trash the room. When you check out, they unblock that money, but there is still a record of it."

"I know a motel that doesn't do that," Annie said. "You will have to give up some luxuries, if you know what I mean, but it's not in a bad part of town or anything like that."

"How would you know about something like that?" I asked.

"Do you think your fiancée has had some flings on the side?" Annie asked. "I know about it because, as a police officer, I have been called out to every place under the sun."

"It's settled then," Lisa said quickly, probably trying to break the tension.

I was relieved that she would be going to a hotel. The thought of sleeping with Annie while Lisa was in the next room was too much for me. I think Annie felt the same way.

It was sometime after nine when Alex showed up. Lisa went out to meet him, and Annie and I followed. He got out of the car, and after the customary greetings, he thanked us for getting Lisa back. He opened the back door and showed us his two children, who were sleeping in their car seats. "Thanks again," Alex said. "It's late, and Lisa says there is a hotel nearby, so we will go there and head back home in the morning."

"I think you will be okay," I said, "but just to be safe, I wouldn't go straight home. Stay on Bill's boat for a couple of days. I doubt Gabriella will be going back there any time soon."

That's where Dad died," he said. "I don't know about that."

"It's up to you," I said, "but lightning doesn't strike twice in the same place."

"Not the best analogy, but I get what you're saying," he said.

"Keep your phone off. When you get somewhere safe, buy a burner phone and call me. I may need your help with something." I said.

"Okay," Alex said before driving off.

Annie said, "I want one of those."

"One of what?"

"Kids."

Chapter 21

I woke up early the following morning and couldn't get back to sleep. I had something on my mind. I got up, made a pot of coffee, and sat at the table with my cup. Annie must have noticed I was up and joined me in the dining room. "Is everything okay," she asked.

"Sure," I said. "I just couldn't sleep. It's 4 a.m. You should go back to bed. I don't want to keep you up."

She stood behind me, put her arms around me, and kissed my cheek. "Something is on your mind," she said. "What is it?"

"Nobody is safe yet," I said. "Parker and Gabriella are still a threat, and I don't know what to do about it. "Plus, they are not just a threat to us. They threaten this whole county now that they have what they were after. They are probably busy right now doing to another innocent person what they did to me."

Annie kissed me on the cheek again and then poured herself a cup of coffee. She sat beside me, took a sip, and put her cup on the table. "I vote we take the bastard down. Him and the psycho bitch."

I nodded, took a sip of coffee, got my phone out, and dialed Alex. It went straight to voicemail. "Alex took my advice and shut his phone off," I said. We should go see him before they leave."

I quickly got dressed, and I took Bruno out for a walk. When I got back, Annie was ready, and we got in the Mustang and headed to the motel. I felt good driving the Mustang, and having Annie next to me was a bonus. When we got to the hotel, we found their vehicle parked in front of unit number two, not far from the office. The parking lot was more than half empty, so we were able to park next to their car. I knocked on the door, and Alex answered sooner than I expected. He must have already been awake. "It's early," he said. "I didn't expect you to come here."

I didn't expect it either, but you did what I said and turned your phone off. We decided this morning that the best defense is a good offense."

"You have a good offense?" he asked.

"Well, no, not yet, but I was hoping to get you on our team," I said.

Alex stepped outside and closed the door. "I would love to help, but I have a family to protect," he said.

"I would not dream of putting you in any more danger than you are already in," I said. "In fact, with your help, I think we can lessen or even eliminate that danger. I want to hack into Parker's security system. Things have changed a lot over the last five years. I don't think I can do it myself."

"John, you should know better than anyone that I am not a hacker," he said.

"No, but you work at a bank where you implement strategies to keep hackers out. You must have learned something," I said.

Alex thought momentarily and said, "All I can do is try. Come on inside."

We followed him into the motel room. The kids were asleep, and Lisa was in the shower. Alex told Lisa we were there and handed her clothes to her. He then got out his laptop and got to work. Lisa came out a few minutes later, and we all said our hellos. She got busy getting the kids ready while Alex was working. A few minutes later, Alex said, "I was able to get in, but everything useful is on an intranet."

"You mean we have to be inside the building to access it?" I said.

"I'm afraid so."

"What if we could access an individual computer hooked up to both the internet and intranet?"

"You would need to get a trojan program onto that computer. How would you do that?"

"I don't know," I said. "I'll figure something out. Do you think you can write it?"

"Probably, but I will need time to research it," he said. "As I said, I'm not a hacker."

"Do what you can when you are safely back in Florida," I said. "I will work on how I can plant it on my end."

Annie and I got back in the car and decided to go out for breakfast. We stopped at a place near the motel. This place had a lot of healthy choices, and Annie ordered granola with fruit and yogurt. I went old school and ordered bacon and eggs with toast. We talked about a lot of things other than the matter at hand. Mostly we talked about our past together. Annie told me many stories about what she and I did together, none of which I remembered. I was hoping that some of John's memories left behind were of Annie and I, but I did not find any that morning.

Finally, Annie said, "Perhaps we should discuss what we should do next. About how we can eliminate our problem."

"I've been thinking about that," I said. "You told me I worked for a private security company. What's it called?"

"I think it's called O'Neil Protective Services," she said. "It was started several years ago by a former Marine named Conor O'Neil. He lost a leg in Afghanistan and, from what you told me, was bored when he returned to the States. He needed something to do, so he got into the security business. When you left the Army, you needed work. His ad was the first one you inquired about. I never met the man, but you did speak highly of him. I believe you two have much in common."

"Do you think he would help us?" I asked.

"It would be a conflict of interest for him, and I think he takes his responsibility seriously, but I think he will help because, from what you told me, he has good character and will do what is right."

"Do you know how to contact him?"

"I'm afraid not, but I'm sure he's listed," Annie said as she picked up her phone to search. "Here he is," she said as she showed me her phone.

"He's in town," I said. "Can we go see him now?"

"I think we have some time before Bruno needs a walk."

By then, the check was already on the table. I looked at it, figured out the tip, then rounded up and left cash on the table.

We got into the car and headed to the address Annie had found. It was on the other side of town, and traffic was heavy, so it took a little while to get there. Annie told me more stories about our time together during the drive. They seemed like great times, and I wanted desperately to remember them. I said, "I hate that I don't have those memories. I would love to do those things with you again so I can remember."

"I would love that, too," Annie said, "and when we're done, we can make new memories together."

"Like we're doing now?" I asked.

"Fifty years from now, we may think of these days as some of our best," she said.

We arrived at our destination at the edge of town. It was a small standalone building that looked like it was a house at one time. It was in a commercial area, but at the time it was built, a hundred years ago or so, the area was probably very different. I saw a new-looking sign near the street that said O'Neill Protective Services. Another sign with the same words hung above the door, but this one was engraved into wood. It was almost like something you would see in the Old West.

I opened the door, held it for Annie, and walked in behind her. To the left was a doorway that led to a small kitchen. To the right was a large desk. A young black woman sat behind the desk. She was attractive, perhaps in her late twenties, with her hair cut short. I guessed she was also ex-military. She looked up and, when she saw me, said very excitedly, "John! You're okay! What happened? Where have you been?" She didn't wait for a response. She got up, walked around the desk, and hugged me.

"It's a long story," I said.

She looked at Annie and said, "You must be Annie," and hugged her too. This woman liked to hug. "John has talked a lot about you."

"All good, I hope," Annie said.

"Of course. He really loves you," she said. "Oh, where are my manners? My name is Vanessa, but everyone around here calls me Jax."

It's nice to meet you, Jax," Annie said. "How did you get that nickname?"

"I was born and raised in Jacksonville," she said.

"Is Connor in, Jax?" I interrupted.

"I'm sorry, John," she said. "He's in his office." She pointed to a closed door on the left.

"No, I'm sorry," I said. "I interrupted you. I didn't mean to be rude. It's just that we have a lot to do in a short amount of time."

"No worries," she said. "I'm just glad you are well."

"I appreciate that," I said.

I knocked twice on Connor's door and then opened it. "Are you busy?" I asked.

"John, c'mon in," he said as he stood up to shake my hand. He wore long pants, so it was difficult to tell he had a prosthetic leg. His left leg did look slightly thinner, so I assumed that was the one. "It's good to see you. I'm so glad you are okay. This must be your lovely fiancée."

He shook Annie's hand, and she said, "I'm Annie. Nice to meet you."

"Please, sit," he said and motioned to the two chairs in front of his desk.

I sat in the chair next to the window, and Annie sat beside me. Conner sat back at his desk. He was perhaps thirty-five, with wavy red hair parted on the side. He had an unshaven look that seemed to be more common than it was five years before.

"I am happy to see you, John," he said. "What happened to you? We didn't know if you had an accident, walked off the job, or something else."

"It wasn't an accident," I said. "I overheard something I wasn't supposed to, and Parker managed to erase my memory. I have almost no memory of you or anything before the incident."

"Almost?" he said.

"I have some vague, random memories, but that's it," I said.

"How is it even possible to erase someone's memory, and how do you know you overheard something if you have no memories?" he said.

"It's hard to explain, but they have a machine capable of messing with people's memories. It is what we were hired to protect. I also found this," I said, pulling out my phone and bringing up the video of Parker and General Rafferty. I set it on the desk and waited for him to watch it.

When the video ended, he looked at me and said, "This is some serious shit. I always considered Parker to be unscrupulous, but this seems downright criminal. Have you gone to the authorities with this?"

"Not yet," I said. "I let them know I have it, so, for now, I think they will be reluctant to kill me, but I won't be safe until they are stopped."

"How did you even get that video, and if he wanted you dead, why didn't he kill you instead of erasing your memory?" Connor said.

"How I got the video is a long story. As far as them not killing me, it is because they needed me alive to get something important that I had. Some of his people, including his girlfriend, kidnapped someone I care about to get it. Now that he has it, he doesn't want loose ends."

"That's pretty vague," Connor said.

"I know," I said. "It's best you don't know everything for your own good. I just need you to trust me."

"Okay," he said. "I will help if I can. What can I do for you?"

"We need access to their computer system. The only way to do it is to have someone on the inside plant a trojan program on one of their computers," I said.

"I'm sorry, John," he said. "Parker canceled his contract with us the day after you went missing. He said trust was compromised, but he wouldn't elaborate. I had no idea what he was talking about, but now I see. He must have hired another agency, or maybe he hired people directly."

"That's disappointing," I said. "I guess we will have to figure something else out."

Annie and I got up, said our goodbyes, and left his office. We almost reached the door when Connor called to us from his office doorway, "Hey! I have an idea." He motioned for us to come back into his office, which we did.

"Can that trojan program be put in an email?" he said.

I thought for a moment and said, "I believe so, but someone on their end would have to open the attachment. That is highly unlikely, given they would be trained to be suspicious."

"What if the email comes from a trusted source?" he said.

"What are you getting at?" I said.

"I was just about to send Parker my final invoice. It is something that I have been sending him once a month since we started working with him. Can it be embedded into the invoice?"

"That's a great idea," I said. I picked up a pen and piece of paper from Connor's desk and wrote down Alex's email. "Can you send the invoice to this email? It is someone that is helping us. He should be able to embed the code and send it back to you. When you get it back, don't open it, just attach it to your email and send it off. You should know, though, that this might put you at risk."

I've faced opponents much better than that dipshit Parker," he said.

"Thank you, Connor," I said and picked up one of his business cards. "I'll call you."

We started to leave again, and Connor said, "Oh, I almost forgot. I have your paycheck. Normally it's direct deposited, but we thought you might have quit. If you did, we like to have you pick it up in person so we can go over exit procedures." He opened the drawer and put the check down on his desk in front of me.

"I didn't quit," I said. "I need some time off, but I hope to have a job when everything is settled."

"I will be glad to have you back," Connor said.

I picked up the check, thanked him, and then we headed back to Annie's apartment. On the way, I texted Alex and told him about the email that would be coming.

Once back at Annie's apartment, Annie and I took Bruno for a walk. After he did his business, we were back on the road again. This time we were in Annie's Explorer so that Bruno could come along.

We went back to the same dog-friendly restaurant we were at before. Annie ordered some kind of salad with strawberries and pecans, and I don't know what else. I got a bacon double cheeseburger with fries.

"That stuff will give you a heart attack one day," she said.

"I'll tell you what. If I survive the next two days, I will let you choose what I eat four days a week for the rest of my life."

"That's an interesting offer that I can't pass up. I guess I will need to keep you alive," she said with a smile.

I smiled back and said, "I guess that you will."

I thought about how much my life had improved in such a short time. I felt my future could be bright except for the nagging problem of people wanting me dead. "Now that I have a paycheck, I feel like my life is starting to become normal," I said. "I just don't know how to cash it. I need a bank card and a driver's license, don't I? I don't even know where I do banking."

"I know where your bank is. Do you have your passport with you?"

"Yes."

"Good. We should have enough time to take care of that today. There's not much else we can do now."

Our server put our check on the table shortly after we finished eating. Annie picked it up, handed it to me, and said, "Now that you have a paycheck and are becoming more normal, you can afford to take me out sometimes."

"I seem to remember paying last time."

"Get used to it," she said with a smile.

We drove to the DMV so I could get a replacement driver's license. I thought it would take hours, but I had a new license in my hand in less than 45 minutes. I looked at it and felt like I was well on my way to being normal again. I took out the fake driver's license that Gabby gave me and threw it in the trash on the way out. I didn't need any reminders of her.

We then went to the bank, which also was much better than expected. I got a temporary debit card until the actual one came in the mail. While I was there, I deposited my check and withdrew $300. I still had cash, but I didn't like using the card for anything. I suspected Parker and Gabby had no idea I knew who I was, but just in case, I thought the fewer breadcrumbs I dropped, the better.

It was getting late, so we went back to Annie's apartment. We ordered Chinese food and sat on the sofa together while we ate. When we finished eating, we tried to plan our next move. I opened my laptop and brought up Parker's building on a map. I switched over to satellite view and then zoomed in.

The building was rectangular, with a highway to the left of one of the short sides. A large parking lot took up the front and right sides. Behind the building was a large, grassy area, perhaps a wetland. I couldn't tell from the photo. I could also see a fence enclosing the entire property.

I switched over to the streetside view. I saw a tall fence, with barbed wire on top, more like a military installation than a business. The building itself was five stories tall. I could see a single main entrance in front. I couldn't get a good view from the other three sides. "I don't know how we can get in there," I said.

"Annie looked at it closely and said, "This will be difficult."

"Do you think you can get in as a police officer? Maybe as part of an investigation."

"Not likely," she said. "The building is outside the city limits. I wouldn't have jurisdiction there."

"There must be a way."

I decided to try something else. I had a particular person in mind, so I typed in a name and location and found a match. I got a pen and paper and wrote down the address. I have a person I want to visit in the morning," I said, "but right now, there is something else I want to do."

I set the laptop to the side, leaned over, and kissed Annie. Things got passionate quickly, and we made love there on the sofa. After a while, we made our way into the bedroom, where we made love again.

Chapter 22

I was awakened by my phone ringing. It was still out in the living room. I looked at the clock. It was 5:45 a.m. I figured it was important, so I got out of bed and shuffled across the carpet into the living room. I looked at my phone. It was Alex. "Hello, Alex," I said.

"I think I got it," he said.

My mind was still foggy, and I asked, "What did you get?"

"The program," he said. "I wrote the trojan program. I tried it on myself, and it worked."

"That's great," I said. "Were you up all night?"

"Once I got started, I didn't want to stop."

"Did you send it back to Connor?"

"Not yet. I figured I would tell you first."

"Okay, send it to Connor with instructions on what he should do. Ask him to contact me when he sends it to Parker, and then thank him," I said.

"Will do," Alex said. "Call me when you need me again. I am going to get some sleep."

"Thanks so much, Alex," I said before hanging up.

I took out Connor's business card. I didn't want to call that early, so I typed out a text. "You should have an email soon with the corrected file. Please send it when you can and let me know it is done. Thanks."

I went back into the bedroom and saw Annie sitting up in bed. "Is everything okay?" she asked.

"Alex finished the Trojan program already and is sending it to Connor."

"Things are going pretty well so far," she said, knocking on the headboard.

I was about to get back in bed with Annie, but just then, Bruno came into the room with his tail wagging hard. He looked up at me and barked once. "I guess his needs come before my needs," I said.

"Don't worry," Annie said. "I will take care of your needs, but later. We should get up now anyway."

I put some clothes on and took Bruno for a walk. When Bruno finished his business, we started heading back to Annie's apartment but were distracted by a woman coming out a door a couple of units to the left of Annie's apartment. She was a white woman, maybe early twenties, and obviously pregnant. I guessed she was about five months along or so. She was wearing an oversized maternity shirt and yoga pants but no shoes. She was crying, and the left side of her face was red like someone punched her or slapped her hard.

I started toward the woman when a young white man came out of the apartment. He was fully dressed, wearing blue jeans, a black t-shirt, and a light jacket, unzipped. He also was wearing work boots, like he was heading off to work. "Hey!'" he said to the woman. "Where do you think you're going?"

Just then, I reached the woman and grabbed her arms to stop her. I pointed to her cheek and said, "Did he do that to you?"

She only nodded. I let go of her and looked at the man in a way that could only be described as a look of rage. I started walking toward him, pointed my finger, and said, "What the hell kind of man hits a woman?"

He stopped, reached under his shirt, pulled a gun out of his pants, and pointed it at me. "This is none of your fucking business," he said.

I had lost track of Bruno, but he suddenly made his presence known by grabbing the man's wrist. The gun went off. It missed me by about a foot and struck the hood of a parked car.

The man managed to kick Bruno, not too hard but hard enough to cause Bruno to lose his grip. He then pointed the gun at Bruno. I moved in. I grabbed the man's wrist and twisted it. I heard bones snap. Then the gun dropped to the ground. I turned my body and came back hard with an elbow to the man's right temple. He fell to the ground, hitting the sidewalk hard. He then lay there moaning and holding his wrist with his left hand.

I looked up, and several people had come out to see what was happening, including Annie, who was only wearing a pair of workout shorts and a t-shirt with no bra. She had her gun in her hands and pointed it at the man, but he could barely move.

She lowered her weapon and said, "What the hell happened?"

"That lowlife beat on this woman here," I said while pointing at the pregnant woman. "I confronted him, and he pulled a gun on me. Bruno grabbed the arm with the gun, and it went off. He kicked Bruno and tried to shoot him, but I took him down."

Annie bent down to check Bruno for injuries. When she saw none, she patted him and said, "Good Boy!" She stood up, patted me on the cheek, and said, "You're a good boy too. Now go inside, please, and get my phone."

I brought Bruno in and came out with Annie's phone. By then, she was talking to the pregnant woman. I gave her the phone, and she called it in. She asked me to keep an eye on the man and woman and went back inside and quickly finished getting dressed. Before long, several cops, an ambulance, and a social worker arrived on the scene. We gave them our statements, and as soon as it seemed we weren't needed for anything, Annie pulled me away, and we went back inside her apartment.

"You saved that woman from continued abuse. You also saved Bruno from getting shot. You're my hero," she said, and put her arms around me and kissed me."

"Aw, shucks, ma'am."

"Do you think Alex could have done what you did?" she asked.

I had to admit I was much more different from Alex than I thought just a few days ago. I was strong, fast, and confident. It was something I never had as Alex, especially the confidence part. "I think Alex would have either avoided the situation or got himself shot," I said.

"We each have our role in life," she said. "I'm glad you are seeing what yours is."

"What do you mean?"

"I think 'justice' would be the word I'm looking for," she said. "You have always hated seeing injustice. You especially hate when the strong take advantage of the weak."

"Like this morning?"

"Exactly."

"Do you think that's why I feel the need to take down Parker and Gabriella?"

"Probably. I'm just like you. I feel that same need."

I was feeling a little hungry and said, "Right now, I feel the need to eat something."

"I'll make breakfast."

"I'm a little too hungry for granola."

"I planned on making you bacon and eggs for breakfast before everything happened."

"You have bacon?"

"Sure, I like bacon."

"I mean, I looked in your fridge but didn't see bacon," I said.

"I always have some in the freezer and take it out sometimes when you spend the night. I took a package out last night."

Annie cooked up the bacon and made scrambled eggs in another pan. While she was doing that, I brewed a pot of coffee. So much had happened that I didn't have a chance to make coffee earlier. I poured Annie and myself a cup and sat down at the table. A minute later, Annie put the bacon and eggs on plates and sat down next to me.

"I like this better than going out for breakfast," I said.

"I'm happy to cook for you, John, but don't expect it every day. When I am back on the job, you won't see this too much."

"That's okay. I would eat cold pizza every morning if I could do it with you. Besides, I can cook too. I'm not a great cook, but I'm okay."

"I would enjoy an okay breakfast cooked by you," Annie said.

"When everything settles down, I will cook you a nice French toast breakfast. I'll even use whatever health nut bread you would like."

"Health nut bread?"

"You know what I mean."

Annie smiled and said, "I look forward to that."

We finished our breakfast and took Bruno out for another walk before the three of us got into Annie's SUV. "Where to?" she asked.

I gave her the address and said, "It's a VA clinic."

"A VA clinic?" she asked. "Is there something wrong with you?"

"No, there is a doctor there I need to talk to," I said.

The clinic was in a less urban area than I expected. It was also smaller and newer than I expected. It was a single-story, somewhat modern-looking building that reminded me more of a city hall than a clinic. We parked the car and went in. The double sliding glass doors opened to a reception desk straight ahead with a waiting area to the left and right. The young man behind the desk said, "Hello, if you have an appointment, please sign in."

"We don't have an appointment," I said. "We are here to see Dr. Carr."

"I'm afraid she is booked up through next week," he said. "If it's important, Dr. Martin had a cancellation. I can get you in at 2:30."

"You don't understand," I said. "I need to see her on an important private matter. If you can just get her out here, I am sure she will see us."

The man hesitated momentarily and then said, "Just a minute," and got out of his chair and disappeared down a hallway. About two minutes later, he and Dr. Carr emerged and headed toward us. When Dr. Carr got close, she recognized me, and a look of surprise came over her face.

She seemed to be thinking for a moment and finally said, "Alex? What are you doing here?"

"Hello, Doctor," I said. "This is my fiancée, Annie. We need to talk. Privately."

She hesitated and then said, "Follow me." She led us to her office and closed the door. There were two chairs in front of her desk. She motioned for us to sit and then sat behind her desk.

"Okay, what is going on?" she said.

"I was surprised to find you working here," I said. "I thought you worked for Scott Parker."

"Oh no," she said. "I was there at the request of General Rafferty. Parker's company is developing an experimental therapy to help people with traumatic brain injuries. He said you were injured in Afghanistan and needed the treatment. The general told me the project wasn't far enough along to hire medical staff, so they wanted me to monitor your vitals in case something went wrong. Were you not aware of any of this?"

I looked at Annie to see if she was buying her story. She shrugged. I looked back at Dr. Carr and said, "My name is John, not Alex, and I did not have a brain injury in Afghanistan. In fact, I left the army several months ago and was working for a private security company protecting Parker Biosystems."

She looked at me with surprise, even shock, and said, "What are you saying?"

"I'm saying that I heard something I wasn't supposed to. Parker and Rafferty put me in that machine against my will. The machine is capable of planting one person's memories into another person's head. My memories were erased in favor of Alex Neuman's memories. I'm also saying if you are involved in this, you are in a world of shit."

She shook her head and said, "The general told me your brain injuries were causing hallucinations. I think you are having one now."

I took out the driver's license I just got and my passport. I passed them to Dr. Carr. "Look at the names and the photos," I said. "Why do you think Parker called me Alex when I woke up? Look me up on the internet. Find my photo."

Dr. Carr hit several keys on her computer and scrolled. After a minute or so, she looked up and said, "Okay, I believe you are not hallucinating, but what you are telling me is too unbelievable."

"You don't have to believe it," I said. "I just need you to believe that Parker and Rafferty are up to no good. They want to use the device to infiltrate top levels of government, like the presidency."

"I'm afraid General Rafferty was in an accident and suffered a brain injury like you did, or at least like I thought you did," she said.

"What?" Annie blurted out. She looked at me and said, "This woman is full of shit. We can't trust her."

"It's true," said Dr. Carr. "They asked me to help again. I monitored the procedure yesterday evening."

Annie and I looked at each other, and she said, "What happened?"

"They told me it was a car accident," said Dr. Carr.

"Not about that," Annie said. "What happened after the procedure?"

"The general woke up and seemed fine," she said.

"Did he seem different to you?" I asked.

"I don't know," she said. "He seemed about what you would expect from someone after an accident. Why?"

"Did he behave differently than me when I first woke up?" I asked.

"Well, he seemed less confused, like he knew what was going on," she said.

I looked at Annie and said, "I think Parker double-crossed Rafferty and put his memories into the general's brain."

"This isn't a science fiction movie," said Dr. Carr. "You are talking about something that's not possible."

"Are you sure about that? Because it happened to me, and you were a part of it," I said. "Did the general have a head injury?"

"Not that I saw," she said. "I assumed it was on the back of his head where it wasn't visible to me."

"How many car accidents result in a head injury to the back of the head?" I asked.

Dr. Carr was silent for a few seconds and then said, "Son of a bitch! You're right. I can't believe I let myself get used like that."

"Nobody's perfect," I said, "but you can help us now."

"How can I help you?" she asked.

"First, you can tell us where the equipment is that they use for these brain transfers," I said.

"Sure," she said. "It's on the third floor. When you get off the elevator, turn right, and it is the last door on the right."

'Where is it from the stairs?" I said.

"Well, I'm not sure where the stairs are, but it would be . . . let's see . . . the northwest corner of the building," she said.

"Do you think you can get us in there?" I asked.

'I can't even get myself in there," she said. "I was invited. I was on their list when I got to the gate."

'Okay," I said. "Can I get a phone number where I can reach you?"

Dr. Carr picked up one of her business cards, wrote her cell number on the back, and handed it to me. I got out my phone and sent her a text message that read, "Call me if you think of anything else, John."

"Okay, I will," she said. "I must get back to my patients now. I wish you luck. Both of you."

After we left the building, I asked Annie, "Do you believe her?"

"I had my doubts initially, but I think she's telling the truth. Either that or she's a highly skilled actress."

"I agree. I think we should risk trusting her."

When we returned to Annie's place, she went inside, and I took Bruno for a walk. I noticed a newer-looking BMW sedan backed into one of the parking spaces with a man sitting in the passenger seat. It was too far away to see the man clearly, but I made a mental note to keep an eye on the car.

When I opened the apartment door, Bruno entered first and immediately started barking and pulling on the leash. I held him back and pulled out my gun. I stepped inside and saw Annie in the living room with Gabby standing behind her, pointing a gun at her head. I pointed my gun at Gabby but then saw David and the other goon from Lisa's kidnapping to my right, both pointing guns at me. The goon closer to me, the one whose name I didn't know, stepped toward me and pressed his gun against my head. Bruno had stopped barking but was now growling. I assumed he was waiting for a command.

'You people are trespassing," I said. "Leave now, or there will be trouble."

Gabby laughed and said, "You have developed quite a sense of humor since I last saw you. I like this new you. I almost hate to kill you. Almost. Now, be a good boy and drop your gun."

I stood my ground. Gabby said, "We don't want to hurt this pretty young lady, but I swear, I will have no problem putting a bullet in her, just like I did to your father. Put the gun down."

I was out of options, so I dropped the gun. When I did, I saw David relax his posture. I looked at Annie and almost imperceivably nodded. She nodded back. I then grabbed the man's hand that had a gun to my head and swung it to the right. At the same time, I put my right foot back and pressed into the man while using both my hands to force the gun to point toward David. Once there, I used my right hand to press against the man's index finger, which was against the gun's trigger. David had lowered his gun slightly when I put my gun down, but he raised it again and tried to get a clear shot at me. I heard a gun fire, but who's gun? I then saw David clutch his chest and drop to the floor.

I looked up and saw Bruno had Gabby's gun hand in his mouth and was shaking his head and growling. Annie punched Gabby in the face, but she didn't go down. Instead, she backed up a step and then stepped forward again, pulling Bruno with her. As she did, she swung at Annie's head, but Annie ducked and delivered a blow to Gabby's side, which caused her to double over in pain and fall on her ass.

I still had my own problems and backed the man against the wall and started smashing his hand against the corner. After the fourth hit, he dropped the gun. I stepped forward and elbowed the man in the face.

I then heard a shot and a whimper. I looked up and saw Parker standing in the doorway, holding a gun. He just shot Bruno. Now he was moving the gun between Annie and me. He looked at Gabby, whose face and arm were now bloody, and said, "I was wondering what was taking so long."

Just then, something hit me on the back of the head, and everything went dark.

Chapter 23

The next thing I saw was a bright light shining in my eyes. It took me a few seconds, but I realized it was a paramedic. I looked around and saw I was still in Annie's apartment. I sat up and said, "Where's Annie?"

"Whoa," said the paramedic. "You have a head injury. You need to be careful."

Several police officers were in the apartment. One was taking pictures of the body lying near me. The paramedic started checking the back of my head when a husky, middle-aged man wearing a suit came up to me. He said, "How are you feeling, John?"

"I have a bit of a headache," I said. "Where's Annie? Are you in charge here?"

He looked at the paramedic, then back at me, and said, "You know who I am. I'm Captain Kowalski. Are you having trouble remembering?"

The paramedic said, "It's not uncommon with a head injury like this."

"I remember good enough to know you didn't answer my question," I said. "Where's Annie?"

"Annie wasn't here when we got here," he said. "I was hoping you could help us find her."

"Shit," I said. "What about Bruno?"

"Bruno's alive," he said. "We don't know the extent of his injury yet, but he is being taken to his vet as we speak. Now, tell me, what happened here?"

"It was Scott Parker and his people. They took Annie," I said.

"Scott Parker, the businessman?" he asked. "What would he want with Annie?"

"I'm not entirely sure myself," I said. "They should have wanted me."

"You?" he said. "Why you?"

I needed to come up with an explanation that was true but didn't make me look crazy. I said, "The reason I don't remember you, Captain, is not because of this head injury. Up until recently, I worked security at Parker Biosystems. As near as I can piece together, I heard Parker and a General Rafferty planning something nefarious. They have an experimental machine there that they used to essentially scramble my memory. I don't remember anything before a week or so ago."

"Your story is a bit out there," he said. "I'm inclined to believe that you believe It, but if your memory is gone, how do you know what happened?"

"It's a long story we don't have time for," I said. "Annie is probably at Parker's place now. If we don't get her out soon, they will fry her brain like they did to me."

The captain waved over a young officer and said, "Where's Johnson?"

"I think she went with the dog," he said.

"Find her and tell her we need a warrant to search Parker Biosystems." The captain said. He then looked at me and said, "Some judges are easier than others, but we need to come up with something better than the word of a man with a concussion and memory problems."

The paramedic finished wrapping my head and said, "You need to go to the hospital and have that looked at."

"I'm fine," I said. "I'm not going to sit around in a hospital while my fiancée's life is in danger."

"She's one of ours too, you know," Captain Kowalski said. "We have the entire force looking for her."

"I'm sorry. I know you are doing everything you can, but somebody needs to do something you can't."

I stood up and retrieved my father's hard drive. I then found my gun that was still on the floor. I picked it up, and one of the officers said, "Hey, that's evidence. You can't take that."

I said, "It's mine and hasn't been fired." I pulled out the clip to show him it was full.

The captain waved at the officer and said, "It's fine. Let him have it."

I went outside and got into the Mustang, and just sat there. I didn't have a plan. I dialed Alex's number. "Hello, John," he said.

"They have Annie. Are you able to get in yet?" I asked.

"Shit, I'm sorry," he said. "I'm in now. I was going to call you, but I'm still trying to figure out their system."

"Can you disable their security system?" I asked.

"Not that I can see, but I'm still looking," he said.

"What about the cameras? Can you disable them?" I asked.

"I do have access to the cameras, but I haven't had a chance to look at them yet. As of now, I don't see a way to shut them off."

"Okay. Look for anything useful. See if you can determine the number of guards on duty and where they are stationed."

Just then, I heard another call coming in. I looked at the number. It was Dr. Carr. "I have another call, Alex," I said. "Call me when you know more."

I hung up with Alex and picked up the call. "Hello, Dr. Carr," I said.

"Hello, John," she said. "I thought you would want to know I got a call from Parker. He wants me to help with another patient tonight."

That confirmed my fear. "It's Annie," I said. "They kidnapped her and are going to use their machine on her. They're tying up loose ends. I hate to say it, but you are also a loose end, Doctor. What time are you supposed to be there?"

"I told them I can be there at seven," she said. "Should I tell them I can't make it?"

"You should go," I said. "I suspect they only needed you at first because they weren't confident in the safety of their device. They used it twice without a problem. Maybe more times than that. I don't think they need a doctor there anymore, but they want you there so they can take care of you afterward."

"That sounds like a good reason for me to cancel," she said.

"I agree. My first instinct would be to stay far away from there. Unfortunately, you know too much," I said. "They will get you one way or another. I know it's risky, but isn't it better to get them first?"

After several seconds of silence, she said, "Okay. I will help in any way I can, but you have to level with me. I want to know everything you know about this machine."

I told her the whole story. I told her about my father and his experiments. I told her about Gabby and everything that happened since I woke up that day. I also told her about Annie and how important she was to me. When I was done, she didn't say I was crazy or anything like that. She just said, "Okay, what's the plan?"

"Do you have a gun?" I asked.

"Of course," she replied. "I was in the Army as a doctor. I learned to fight, but I was never in combat."

"At least you know how to use a gun. Hopefully, you won't need it, but it's better to have it, just in case," I said. "Let's meet somewhere close to Parker's building at 6:30 to go over the plan. Do you know a good place?"

"Well, there's a Carrabba's nearby," she said. "I don't know the address, but it shouldn't be hard to find. We can meet in the parking lot behind the building."

"Okay, I'll see you then."

I hung up and checked the time on my phone. It was 4:15. The cops were still in Annie's apartment, and I didn't know what to do, so I just started the car and drove. I ended up at a small diner. I was about to order a hamburger but thought about Annie. If I lived through this, she was going to help me make better choices, but what if she didn't live through this? I decided on a grilled chicken salad and a bottle of spring water.

When I was almost done eating, Alex called. "Hello, Alex. Tell me you have some good news."

"I think I am fairly comfortable with how everything works. I did not find a way to shut the alarm system. However, I can do a soft reset from here. That should shut everything down for a short time, including the cameras." He said.

"How long do you think it will take for the cameras to come back up?" I said.

"I can't know that from here, but I wouldn't count on much more than ninety seconds," he said.

"That will have to do. What about security?"

"It looks like one guard at the gate, two at the entrance, two on the third floor, and whoever is in the control room. There are no cameras there."

"Okay. Shit is going down at around seven. I'll need your help."

"I'll be here."

"Thanks, Alex. Let me know if anything changes between now and seven."

I hung up and asked for my check. I had a stop to make. While I waited, I checked my phone for nearby hardware stores.

The hardware store I found was mostly on the way to the rendezvous point. I went inside and found what I needed: a roll of duct tape and the largest zip strips I could find. When I checked out, the young man at the register laughed and said, "Are you planning to kidnap someone?"

"Yes," I said. "Your mother." The smile disappeared from his face as I grabbed my bag and walked out.

I pulled into the Carrabba's parking lot ten minutes early. Dr. Carr had not arrived yet, so I called Alex. "Hello, John," he said.

"Alex, are you still connected?" I asked.

"I'm still connected," he said.

"Good. I'll call you back shortly."

Dr. Carr showed up a few minutes later. She was driving a sleek blue sedan that I later learned was a Tesla Model S. She parked next to me on the left, and I went out to meet her. She buzzed the passenger window down and said, "Hello, John."

"Hi, Dr. Carr," I said. "Nice car."

"Thanks," she said. "You can call me Sarah."

"Okay, Sarah," I said. "Just a minute. I need to get something out of the car."

I opened the door and grabbed the bag from the hardware store and the hard drive before locking the car. I shoved the hard drive into my front pocket. It was somewhat of a tight fit, but I didn't want to carry it. I got into the passenger seat of Sarah's car and was a little surprised by what I saw. It looked like I had jumped way more than five years into the future. There were no controls on the dashboard except for a large computer screen in the center.

"This is really something," I said.

"It takes a little getting used to, but I like it," she said.

"It looks like Alex can buy us some time once we get in, but I must admit that I am still working out how to get past the guard at the gate without setting off any alarms," I said.

"I've already figured that one out," she said. "The last couple of times, the guard checked the inside of my car and the trunk, but there is one place he didn't check." She pulled up a menu on the computer screen, tapped it a couple of times, and the hood unlatched.

"The hood?" I asked. "You want me to climb into the engine compartment?"

"There's no engine," she said. "This is an electric car. Go on. Take a look."

I got out of the car, opened the hood, and saw an open space where an engine would typically be. Sarah had also gotten out of the car and was finding amusement in the look on my face. "Where's the motor?" I said.

"It's there, behind all that plastic. It's just a lot smaller than an engine, so there is extra space up here," she said.

"It still looks too small for someone my size," I said.

"It won't be comfortable, but you should fit," she said. "Try it."

168

Reluctantly I folded myself in the small space, and Sarah closed the hood most of the way to make a point, but she didn't latch it. It was a tight squeeze, but I managed to fit myself inside with not much room to spare. She then opened it, and I climbed back out.

"Okay," I said, "but I want to get close before I climb into that thing again."

We drove away, and Sarah pulled over just before we got to within line of sight of the guard shack. I climbed back into what she called a "frunk," which I assumed was a "front trunk." I made sure my gun and phone were easily accessible, just in case.

We drove for less than a minute, and then I felt the car stop. I heard a muffled conversation, and we were moving again less than sixty seconds later. After another thirty seconds or so, the car came to a stop, and I heard the latch open. I pushed up the hood and climbed out.

Chapter 24

I looked around. The parking lot only had a few cars. I guessed there wasn't a second shift. Sarah had parked a little away from the main door, next to one of the company vans. It gave us cover from any cameras pointing at the parking lot. I closed the hood and grabbed the bag from the front seat.

"Wait a minute," I said. I got my phone out and dialed Alex.

"Hello," he said.

"Are you still ready?" I asked.

"Yes," he said.

I looked at Sarah and said, "Go ahead of me. Do what you would normally do. I will follow in ninety seconds."

I told Alex, "Wait ninety seconds and reboot the system."

Sarah walked to the main doors and went inside. I counted down the time in my head as I watched her. I saw her speak briefly with the security guards and then walk past them.

When I counted to ninety, I stepped out of the shadow of the van and approached the building. I walked inside and up to the desk where the two security officers were sitting. I pleasantly said, "Hi, I have an appointment to see Mr. Parker."

Both men briefly glanced down at their computer screens. When they looked back up, I had my gun out and was pointing it at them. I said, "Very slowly, pull out your guns and set them on the counter. If your fingers go anywhere near the trigger, you will lose them."

Both men hesitated, and I said, "I have very little time. I will shoot you if that speeds things along."

Both men took out their guns and set them in front of me. I saw a garbage can near the end of the counter, so I dropped them both in the trash. I then pulled out a couple of the large zip ties and told the man on the left to sit down, and told the man on the right to zip tie his hands behind his back. Tight.

Once he did that, I tore off two pieces of duct tape and told him to place the tape over the two cameras behind the security desk. He had to stand on a chair, but he managed. I figured once the cameras came back online, that would confuse the man in the camera room, at least temporarily.

I instructed the man to sit on the other chair, and I zip-tied his arms behind his back. I then zip-tied their legs to the chairs and put duct tape over their mouths. I pushed the chairs forward so that, at least from a distance, they would look like they were on duty.

I headed to the stairs on the north end of the building and climbed to the third floor. I cracked the door open and saw the room I was looking for. Unfortunately, two armed guards were standing at the door. I closed the door and thought for a moment.

I reopened the door and walked through. The guards immediately pulled their guns and pointed them at me. I continued to walk toward them and said, "I'm so glad I found you. I was working late on the second floor, and a crazy man showed up with a gun."

I continued to advance and said, "He insisted on seeing Parker. I told him he was on the fourth floor."

When I got close enough, I kicked straight up and hit the hand of the guard on the right. His gun flew out of his hand and hit the ceiling before dropping to the floor. I immediately swung my right arm to the left and hit the second guard's wrist with my forearm, causing him to drop the gun. I kicked the first guy in the solar plexus and elbowed the second guy hard on the side of the head just above his ear. He went down, but the first guy was trying to straighten up. I stepped toward him, put my hand on his head, and shoved it against the wall. He went down too. I figured they would be out for a bit, so I didn't bother tying them up. I then picked up their guns and tucked them into my waistband, behind me and out of sight.

I took my gun out and opened the door. Parker was standing in front of me and to the left. The guy who knocked me out in Annie's apartment was beside him, pointing a gun at me. Straight ahead, I saw Annie lying on a machine like what my father used to scan my brain. Gabby was next to her with a gun against her head. To my right was Sarah. Behind her and to her left was one of Parker's guards with a gun pointed at her back.

Parker took a step forward and said, "Welcome, Alex. We've been expecting you."

"John," I said. "The name's John."

"Forgive me, John," he said. "Now, please drop the gun before someone gets hurt."

"I would suggest that you tell your people to drop their guns or that someone will be you," I said.

"I'm not afraid of dying," Parker said. "Are you?"

"I suspect you'll live on as a general."

"I didn't give you enough credit. You are smarter than I thought and way more of a pain in the ass."

"I knew you had no morals, but screwing over your partner like that is lower than low."

"Well, you know, plans change. I might as well tell you because you won't repeat it. The original plan was to replace members of Congress who would rather spend money on social programs than on keeping this country safe."

"I assume keeping this country safe involves a lot of Parker Biosystems contracts."

"Of course," Parker said, "but that was nothing compared to the real prize."

"The presidency," I said.

"Rafferty changed his mind and decided against the idea. He liked the guy. Now he's for it. Tonight, he will convince the president that preserving his memories would greatly benefit the country and his legacy."

"I'm afraid I can't let you do that."

Parker laughed and said, "Put the gun down. I won't ask again. I did have plans for these two lovely ladies here, but if I must kill one of them, I will."

I knew killing Annie, or Sarah, would be nothing more than a slight inconvenience for Parker, so I slowly set the gun on the floor at my feet.

"Now, kick it toward me."

I did what he said and kicked the gun toward him.

"Tell me," I said. "If you knew I would come for you, why didn't you just shoot me at Annie's apartment?"

"Look at everything you've accomplished while hindered with the memories of a computer nerd. Imagine what you could do with my memories."

"So, you just want me for my body. I'm sorry, but you're not my type."

"Gabby told me you developed a sense of humor. I see she was right."

"I was unconscious. You could have just taken me with you then," I said.

"It was one thing to walk out with your girlfriend, quite another to carry your unconscious body past several witnesses. It was easier to have you come to us."

Just then, the room went dark. Out of what seemed like pure instinct, I reached behind me and pulled the two guns out that I had taken from the security guards. From memory, I fired the gun in my left hand once and the gun in my right hand twice. After a few seconds, the lights came back on, and I saw the two men on the floor. I also saw Gabby on the floor. She was clutching her chest and moaning.

Parker knelt next to her and said, "Gabby! Oh my God!" He looked at me and yelled, "Call her an ambulance!"

I put the guns back in my pants and looked around for a phone when Gabby said, "It's too late. But don't worry, my dear. This is not the end of our story." She then took her last breath and died.

Parker put his arms around her and started weeping. After a few seconds, he looked up at me with pure rage on his face. He stood up, pointed at me, and yelled, "You killed her, you son of a bitch."

He took two steps toward me and attempted to punch me in the face, but I squatted down and punched him in the gut just as his punch sailed over my head. He doubled over in pain and fell to the floor with both hands on his stomach.

I walked over to Annie, looked at Sarah, and said, "Is she okay?"

The doctor moved next to Annie. She checked her eyes, pulse, and breathing and said, "She's been medicated, but she should be okay," she said.

"That's good," I said, and while Parker was squirming on the floor, I picked up my gun and put it in its holster. I then picked up the other guns and put them all on a table, including the two in my waistband, far from Parker's reach.

There was a gurney in the room. I moved it close to Annie and said, "Help me move her onto this." The two of us picked her up and put her on the gurney. I then pushed her away from the machine.

"What is the drug that they used to put Annie out? Is it in this room somewhere?" I asked.

Sarah looked around and found a cabinet with an assortment of bottles. She pulled one out and said, "Here it is."

"Good," I said. "I need enough to put him out," and pointed to Parker, who was still on the floor clutching his stomach.

Sarah found a needle and extracted some of the drug. She then handed me the needle. "That should be enough to put him out for a half hour or so," she said.

I took the needle and walked over to Parker. I set the needle down and said, "What did Gabby mean when she said it wasn't the end of your story?"

Parker laughed and said, "You can kill us, but we will live on."

"You mean in General Rafferty?" I said.

"And his wife," he said and laughed again. "Maybe others, too."

I picked up the needle and jabbed it in his arm. "Shit!" he said. "What is that?"

"Just a little something to help you sleep," I said. Before I finished the sentence, he was out.

I dragged him close to the machine and asked Sarah, "Can you help me get him up here?"

He was heavier than Annie, but we managed to get him up and onto the machine.

"What are you going to do?" Sarah asked.

"He is going to get a taste of his own medicine," I said.

I went to the computer terminal and noticed the program was already running. I saw a big green button at the bottom of the screen that said, "Run." I looked around and found an external device for plugging in hard drives. There was room for five hard drives, but only one was plugged in. I pulled it out and saw the word "Gabby" written with a black marker on it. I set it down, took the hard drive out of my pocket, and plugged it in. I then clicked the "Run" button.

The machine came to life. Lights started flashing, and it started making a loud thumping noise as Parker's head slowly moved toward the scanner. Parker stopped moving when his head reached the correct position, but the noise continued. After a minute or two, the platform reversed, and the noise stopped.

I looked at Sarah and said, "We don't have much time. Can you wake him?"

She looked through the medicine cabinet and found a bottle of something. She extracted some into a needle, held it up, and said, "This should wake him, but there are risks."

"We don't have much choice," I said. "Go ahead."

She injected the contents of the needle into Parker's arm and then stood back and watched. His eyes opened, and he blinked several times. He looked around and said, "What happened? Where am I? What is this place?"

I looked at him and said, "What is your name?"

"Bernard Neumann," he said. "Who are you?"

"Oh my God," Sarah said. "I admit I had doubts, but this is incredible."

"What is she talking about?" said the man formally known as Parker.

"I'm sorry," I said. "I would like to break this to you gently, but there is no time. It is five years later than you think. After you invented a machine to extract people's memories, you went to work with a man named Scott

Parker. He had the money and resources to help you design a machine to reverse the process and implant memories into people. The device worked, but you learned what Parker had in store for it, and you disappeared with the technology. Since Parker already had the memories of Alex, your son, he implanted his memories into another person's body. He hoped that Alex could help find you. To make a long story short, I'm Alex".

"That's ridiculous," he said. "You are not Alex. What's going on here?"

"Technically, I'm John, but I have Alex's memories," I said. "There's more. Your memories are now in Scott Parker's body. Think about it. The last thing you remember is having your brain scanned." There was a mirror on the desk. I picked it up and showed him his face.

"You can freak out later. Right now, I need you to be Scott Parker. You are the boss here. I pointed to the people on the ground. These people are your employees, and they tried to kill you, but I and Dr. Carr here saved you." I pointed at Sarah. "Do you think you can sell it?"

He took a deep breath and said, "I'll do what I have to do."

I quickly explained to him what happened and told him what to say. It was hard to think of Scott Parker as my dad. I'm sure he was having a hard time with it too, but he didn't show it at that moment.

We walked out into the hallway as the two guards were waking up. "What the hell are you two doing?" Dad said. "My own people tried to kill me, and you men are out here napping."

One pointed at me and said, "It was him."

"He was the one who saved me," Dad said. "Your services are no longer needed here," he told them. "Now go home. On the way out, untie the two men downstairs and tell them they are no longer needed either."

After they left, Dad leaned against the wall, took a deep breath, and sighed. He said, "This is too much for me to process right now."

"We need to check on Annie," I said, and we returned to the room. She was still unconscious. I put her hand in mine, and her eyes slowly fluttered open. She looked at me and said, "I knew you would come for me."

We hugged, and I said, "I couldn't bear the thought of Gabriella in your head," I said.

Annie tried to sit up. I helped her. She looked around and saw the bodies on the floor, including Gabby. "I can't say she didn't deserve it," she said.

She then noticed Parker standing behind me and became angry. "What the hell is he doing here? He should be on the floor with the rest of the trash."

"Brace yourself," I said. "Parker is gone. This is Bernie, Alex's dad. In a way, my dad too."

"What?" she said. "You put Parker in the machine? That was genius and quite ironic."

I turned and said, "Dad, this is Annie, my fiancée."

He said, "Annie, I am very pleased to meet you."

"Likewise," she said hesitantly.

Just then, my phone rang. It was Alex. I answered and said, "We're okay. Thanks for your help."

"I'm so relieved," he said. "When the cameras came back on, I saw it was a trap, but it was too late to warn you. After you put your gun down, I feared the worst."

"I should have bought an earpiece and kept you on the line."

"Lesson learned," he said.

"Did you turn off the lights?" I asked.

"Yes. I couldn't think of anything else. It was a Hail Mary pass."

"There is something you should know," I said. "The hard drive we got from Dad's safety deposit box contained his memories from five years ago. Those memories are now in Scott Parker's head."

"Oh, Jeez," he said. "This just gets weirder and weirder."

"You should talk to him," I said. "I think he could use a familiar voice."

I put the phone on speaker and said, "It's Alex."

Dad said, "Alex? Is that you?"

"It's me, Dad. How are you holding up?"

"I've had better days," he said. "It is so good to hear your voice."

"It's good to hear from you too, Dad," Alex said.

"When I did that brain scan of myself, I never in my wildest dreams thought this could be the result."

"John went through what you are going through now," Alex said. "Lean on him. He can help you."

"I will," said Dad. "I'll call you when I am more settled."

I took the phone off speaker and said, "Alex, you should be safe to go home now. Parker and Gabby are still technically out there, but you should not be a concern for them anymore."

"Does Dad know what happened to him yet?" he asked.

"Not yet, but I will tell him," I said.

"We'll head home in the morning," he said. "Thanks for everything."

I hung up and looked at Annie. "We need to explain this to the police."

"I can help with that," she said.

"Good," I said, "but before you do, I have a few things I want to do."

"Dad," I said, "do you think you can get this thing to scan memories?"

He went to the computer screen, opened a new menu, clicked a couple of buttons, and said, "It's good to go."

"So, it will just scan and nothing more, right?" I said.

"Don't worry," he said. "It is set to scan."

I removed Dad's hard drive and located one marked "Scott." I then connected it to the system. I opened a file explorer window and formatted the hard drive. "I said, "Now we won't see any more copies of Scott Parker."

"How many do you think are out there now?" Annie said.

"Just one, I hope."

I lay on the machine and said, "Okay, Dad, let's do this."

He started the machine up, and I was slowly pulled into the device. After several minutes, the machine shut down, and I got off it. I unplugged the hard drive, then found Gabby's hard drive, connected it, and repeated what I did to Parker's hard drive. Annie saw what I was doing and said, "No! I'm not getting in that thing again."

"It's perfectly safe. I did it first so you could see."

"I don't think so."

"I will accept if you say no, but it would mean a lot to me if you did this," I said.

She thought for a moment and then said, "Okay, I will do it for you, but if I turn into Psycho Bitch you will have to live with it.

Annie got on the machine, and Dad started it up. When it finished, Annie sat up, and I said, "Gabby, is that you?"

"Very funny," she said as she hopped off the table.

I went to the computer that controlled the machine and set password protection on it. I wanted to dismantle the thing and erase everything related to it, but I thought there might be one more use for it before I destroyed it.

I unplugged Annie's hard drive and put both drives in the cabinet under the machine.

I asked Sarah to prepare two more injections for putting people to sleep.

"Who do you want to put to sleep?" she asked.

There are still a couple of pretenders out there," I said.

She did what I asked, and I put the two syringes on top of the machine, out of sight.

Chapter 25

Annie called the police, and they came in droves. We waited in the lobby as her captain and several members of the Fredericksburg police station showed up, as well as about a dozen sheriff's deputies. Annie's captain and fellow cops were all happy to see her alive. They showed up first, followed by the sheriff's deputies a few minutes later. One of the deputies said this was not the jurisdiction of the Fredericksburg Police Department.

"Don't you lecture me about jurisdiction," the captain said. "One of my officers was kidnapped. That makes it my jurisdiction." The deputy shut up after that.

A couple of the officers and a couple of deputies remained downstairs while everyone else filtered up to the third floor. We all got our stories straight and said that Gabby and the other two men broke into Annie's apartment and kidnaped her to get me to give up evidence against them.

I said I had a video of them using their device on me, but I gave them my only copy to get Annie back, and they erased it. I didn't tell them what the device was capable of because they would not have believed it. I just said it was able to scramble people's memories.

Speaking as Scott Parker, Dad said the machine was supposed to help people remember, but it didn't work as intended. He said the three dead people there and the one at Annie's home were employees who wanted to steal and sell the device. He speculated that it would be worth a lot of money to many unscrupulous people. He said he planned on destroying it and the plans for it to keep it out of the hands of bad people.

Explaining how three people ended up dead was a little more complicated. I wanted to keep Alex out of it, so I said they were about to scramble Annie's brain when Dr. Carr elbowed the guy with a gun at her side. I said it distracted everyone enough for me to take them out. I certainly didn't want to say I shot them in the dark. They would have thought I was reckless and crazy. Desperate and lucky would be better words.

182

We all waited in the lobby for the investigation to finish. Fortunately, there were several comfortable chairs for us to sit in. After a while, Annie's captain came down and sat next to her. He put his hand on her arm and said, "I'm happy that you're okay. We were all very concerned. I know it must have been a traumatic experience, and I want you to take your time returning to work."

"Thank you, sir," Annie said. "How's Bruno? Have you heard?"

"He has a bit of recovering to do," he said, "but the vet thinks he will get through it okay. I'm not sure if he will be capable of police work again."

"I think he'll surprise you," she said.

"I look forward to being surprised," he said.

He looked at me and said, "I also want to thank you for what you did. You did what needed to be done to get Annie back safely. I respect you for that, but I must say that I don't buy that cockamamie story you all told. You guys are lucky this is not my jurisdiction." With that, he got up and walked away.

I looked at Annie and said, "I really like your boss."

She just nodded in agreement.

It was midnight when the last deputy left. Sarah said she needed to get some sleep and asked if we could use a ride back to my car. I accepted, so she dropped us off at the Carrabba's parking lot. Dad sat in the back, and Annie got in the front with me. I turned to look at Dad and said, "You know, you are a billionaire now. I'm sure you have a huge house around here somewhere. Do you want us to find it?"

"Perhaps tomorrow," he said. "Right now, I want to spend some time with my second favorite son and his beautiful fiancée."

"You're funny, Dad," I said. "That's a good one."

When we got to Annie's apartment, I asked Dad if he had Parker's phone on him. He checked his pockets and pulled out a smartphone. He handed it to me. It unlocked using a fingerprint, so I handed it back to Dad and said, "Put your finger on the scanner."

He touched the bottom of the phone, and it unlocked for him. He then handed it back to me, and I opened the phone app. I looked through his contacts and found General Rafferty's number.

"I know it's late," I said, "but we need to call General Rafferty." I then explained to Dad how the general was involved and that he was now Parker, and his wife was probably Gabriella.

"This is enough to make a person's head spin," he said.

"I know," I said, "but we need to tell him there was trouble tonight, and he should hold off before getting the president involved. Are you okay with talking to him?"

"Sure. Give me the phone."

I handed him the phone. He hit dial and waited. I put my ear close so I could hear. After 15 seconds, Rafferty answered and said, "It's after midnight. What is it?"

"I'm sorry to wake you, but there's been an incident," Dad said. "Gabby's been killed, along with three of our men."

"Shit!" he said. "How did you let this happen?"

"I didn't 'let' anything happen," Dad said. "I'm calling because we need to put the brakes on this thing with the president until things cool down."

"No," Rafferty said. "We've come too far to stop now. The thought of immortality has him licking his chops. We need to strike now while we have the chance."

I won't debate you on this," Dad said. "Give things a week to cool down. Then we'll get him." He hung up without waiting for a reply.

We were all tired, so we gave Dad the second bedroom and went to bed. I got in bed with Annie, put my arm around her, and immediately dozed off.

I woke up before 7 a.m. The room was bright, and I tried to go back to sleep but couldn't, so I got out of bed. I put my clothes on and went to the kitchen to make coffee. Dad was already sitting at the dining room table, drinking coffee. "I made a pot. I assumed you would want some," he said.

"You assumed right," I said as I poured myself a cup. I brought it over to the table and sat across from Dad.

"We are quite the pair," he said. "Father and son and not even related."

"Family is not defined by blood," I said. I needed to tell him what happened to him, but I was reluctant. Finally, I said, "Dad, I have some unpleasant news."

He took a sip of his coffee, put his cup down, and said, "Are you going to tell me that the real me is dead?"

"How did you know?"

"I didn't. The fact that the version of me that you have is five years old sort of gave it away. How long have I been gone?"

"Not long," I said. "The dead woman you saw yesterday shot you. The hard drive with your memories was in your safe deposit box. You destroyed all the data at Parker's lab, so I assume you had that at your house since before you went to work for him."

"Before I died, did I tell you how sorry I am for not being there for you when I should have been?"

"You did make that clear, Dad," I said. "It's okay. You loved Mom, and you wanted to help others like her. I respect that."

185

Just then, Annie walked in and said, "I'm sure glad you made coffee. I can use some."

I got up, pulled out a chair between Dad and me, and motioned for her to sit, "I'll get your coffee, my dear."

I made Annie a cup of coffee, put it in front of her, and sat down again.

Annie said, "I'd like to see Bruno this morning. The vet opens at eight."

"I am up for that," I said. "I miss having him around."

We all grabbed our coffees and went into our respective bedrooms to shower and get ready. I realized that Dad had no clean clothes, so I found something of mine that he could wear.

We arrived at the vet a little after eight and were ushered into one of their exam rooms. I expected Bruno to be in a kennel or something, but he was lying on an exam table. He was on his side with a bandage wrapped around his abdomen. His eyes were open, and his tail started wagging when he saw us, but he didn't lift his head.

Annie went to him and petted his head, and scratched his ears. She looked at the vet tech that brought us into the room and asked, "How is he?"

The vet tech was a young woman that was probably fresh out of college. She said, "He is doing better than expected. He was very lucky the bullet didn't hit any major organs. He did lose a lot of blood, so we are monitoring him closely. He is lightly medicated to reduce pain and keep him from moving too much, but the vet doesn't want to risk any more medication than necessary right now."

Annie stayed with Bruno for about ten minutes, comforting him and letting him know what a good boy he was. Then the vet came in. She was an older woman with grey hair tied behind her in a ponytail. She said, "Bruno will be fine. He is a fighter."

"Thank you, Doctor," Annie said.

"It is always a pleasure to help our dogs in blue," she said. I want you to know that we all heard what happened to you and are beyond relieved that you are okay."

"Thank you so much," Annie said.

After we left the vet, we headed towards Parker's building. On the way, we stopped for breakfast. We talked about how Dad could make Parker Biosystems a force for good. We decided that the ability to record memories would be a good tool for measuring the rate of decline, but the machine that could replace a person's mind had to be destroyed, along with all the research data.

We saw two men in Army uniforms at the gate when we got to Parker's building. One was inside the guard house, and the other outside. Annie was driving. She rolled down her window and said, "What is going on?"

The soldier said, "This business is under lockdown until further notice. Only authorized personnel beyond this point."

Annie said, "I have the owner of the company with me."

Dad buzzed his window down and said to the soldier, "I'm Scott Parker, the owner of this company. Who's in charge here?"

"That would be General Rafferty," he replied.

"Well, you tell General Rafferty that I demand to be let into my own building," Dad said.

The soldier said, "I need to see all your identifications."

We all passed our IDs to the soldier, who took them into the guard house. He was on the phone for about thirty seconds and then returned and handed back our IDs. He said, "You are clear to proceed." He stepped back and motioned to the other soldier who raised the gate.

The parking lot was nearly empty except for a few Army vehicles and company vehicles. We parked and went through the main entrance. General Rafferty, or the new Scott Parker, was waiting inside for us. Dad said, "What the hell is going on here? What are you doing?"

A couple of soldiers were nearby, so Rafferty said, "Let's walk." We walked to the far side of the lobby, and he said, "I did what needed to be done. The president and his wife will be here this evening, and tomorrow we will have the White House. Whatever happened here last night is not going to prevent that."

Dad looked at me, and I figured going along with him would be wise, at least for a while, so I said, "I hope you know what you are doing."

Rafferty looked at Dad and asked, "Is he one of us now?"

"Yes," Dad said, "and she's Gabby."

Annie smiled at the general and said, "Hello, Scott. I didn't recognize you with all those stars."

"Hello, Gabby," Rafferty said. "Are you three here to support me or oppose me on this? You seem overly cautious. That is not like us."

"You know as well as I do that I am cautious when caution is called for," Dad said. "Maybe you inherited some of the general's recklessness."

"Whether you agree or not, the presidency will be ours tonight. I've got the third floor sealed off, but you are free to use our office," Rafferty said before walking away.

"Where is 'our' office?" Dad asked.

Annie and I both shrugged, and Annie said, "Maybe, there's a directory."

We went to the elevator, and sure enough, there was a directory on the wall. Parker's office was number 501 on the top floor. We got in the elevator, and Annie pressed "5."

It was a corner office with windows on two sides. The left windows overlooked a grassy area and the highway behind it. The right windows overlooked a larger grassy area with trees behind that. The office was about twice the size of a typical office, but it wasn't as big or extravagant as I expected. There was a large wooden desk to the right with two chairs in front of it. There was a sofa against the left window and a bookcase on each side of the doorway. I got the impression that Parker did real work while he was in his office.

I sat at Parker's desk and tapped a key on the keyboard. The screen came up and asked for a fingerprint. I looked around and saw a fingerprint reader to the right of the keyboard.

"Dad, I need your fingerprint," I said.

He came around next to me, placed his finger on the scanner, and the desktop came up. I clicked on a shortcut icon labeled "Current Projects." A message came up that read, "No Network Access."

There was another icon that read, "Security." I clicked on it, and the same message came up, "No Network Access."

I said, "It looks like Rafferty has turned off our internal network."

"Why would he do that?" Dad asked.

"I think I know," Annie said. "Do you know how you retained some of John's traits, like his badassness? Maybe the same thing happened to Rafferty."

"Badassness?" I said.

"You know what I mean," she said. "I think the general does not enjoy sharing power. He's asserting his dominance over other versions of himself or at least other perceived versions."

"That makes sense," I said. "So, what do we do to get that power back?"

"Right now, I'm not sure," she said. "He seems to be holding all the cards."

"Can we get a message to the president?" Dad asked.

"Have you ever tried to contact the president?" I asked.

"I see your point," he said. "It's not like Abraham Lincoln is president, and citizens could just walk into the White House."

We threw some ideas around for about ten minutes, and then the door opened, and a middle-aged woman stepped inside. She was tall and fit, in her late thirties, I guessed. She had shoulder-length, dark brown hair and wore tight-fitting jeans and a low-cut blouse. She looked at me with disdain, walked over to Dad, and slapped him across the cheek.

"That's for letting me get killed," she said. "How could you do that?"

We all realized then that she was Gabby reincarnated as Rafferty's wife.

"It wasn't like I planned it," Dad said. "Besides, if you had taken care of him along with his father, none of this would have happened."

"It was your idea to put him in the body of an Army Ranger," she said. "Not the smartest thing you ever did."

"We had no choice, and you know that," Dad said.

"I think we need to stop bickering and focus on the prize," I said.

She looked at me and said, "I should kill you for what you did."

"Gabby," I said. "I thought you loved me."

"I think we can lose one of you. Three is more than I can handle," she said.

Annie spoke up and said, "This one is mine, and you will keep your hands off him."

"Are you supposed to be me?" Gabby said.

"I don't even know who you are," Annie said.

"Can we all please work as a team?" Dad said. "You all need to get used to using your real names. I'll start. I'm Scott Parker."

"I'm John Thomas," I said.

"I am Annie Hansen", Annie said.

We all looked at Gabby, who said, "Alright! Alright! I'm Maryanne Rafferty."

I laughed and said, "Maryanne? Not Ginger?"

"I'm glad you were able to keep your sense of humor, John." She put the stress on "John."

Dad interrupted and said, "So what's the plan today? What can we do?"

Gabby said, "Well, the secret service should be here soon to sweep the place. The president and his wife will be in later, around six, to have their memories 'recorded.' There isn't much else we can do but wait."

"I can run the machine," Dad said.

"My husband will do that," she said. She paused and then said, "You know, it's ironic. I waited a long time for you to ask me to marry you, but you never did. The funny thing is I'm married to you now, and you still have never asked."

Annie poked my side and smiled. She said, "My Scott asked me." I'm sure she felt an opportunity to get a little jab in at Gabby, so she took it.

Gabby said, "I have things to do with my husband right now." She made sure she stressed the word "husband." She then turned and walked out the door.

191

Chapter 26

We ran out of ideas, so we just hung out in Parker's office until something came up. It came up about an hour later when Dad got a call from Rafferty. He put it on speakerphone and said, "Hello."

Rafferty said, "The Secret Service is here. I want to show the head guy that the machine is safe, but it is password protected. Did you do that?"

Dad looked at me, confused. I motioned that he should go with it. He said, "Yes. I want to make sure I'm involved in what goes on at my business. I was concerned that you were not the team player I had hoped we would all be, and I was right."

The general hung up the phone, and I said, "That didn't go the way I expected."

"I think we should all leave here while we still can," Annie said.

"I agree," Dad said.

"Okay," I said. "We can probably do more from outside anyway."

We made it down to the lobby, but four soldiers stopped us. One said, "I'm sorry, but we were ordered to detain you."

"We are not in the Army, and we've done nothing wrong," I said. "You have no authority over us."

"We have our orders," the soldier said.

They led us down the hall and put us in the men's bathroom. There was no lock on the door, but two soldiers were posted just outside. We looked around for another way out, but there were no windows, and the air vents were far too small for a person to fit into.

"What do we do now?" Annie asked.

"I have no idea," I said.

"Maybe we can call someone," Dad said. "They didn't take our phones."

We all took out our phones, and Annie said. "I'm not getting a signal."

"Me neither," Dad said.

I looked at my phone and said, "They must have one of those cell phone jammers. That's why we still have our phones."

We discussed what we would say when the time came, and that time came sooner than expected. Five minutes after being put in the bathroom, the door opened, and General Rafferty walked in. He said, "I'm sorry about the treatment, but I need that password, and you will give it to me."

Dad said, "I Resent this treatment. We are all on the same team here."

"Are we?" asked Rafferty.

"Yes, we are," I said. "We are just not sure you are a team player."

"C'mon," Dad said. "You know that I, or we, wouldn't be happy as a glorified bodyguard. We don't need more of us than necessary to reach our goal. We will show this Secret Service agent that the machine is safe, and that is all we need to do. I will unlock it, but I will also run it. That's the deal."

The general thought for a moment and then said, "Fine. Let's go."

He led us out of the bathroom and to the lobby, where three secret service agents were waiting. The leader was a black man, about fifty years old. His colleagues were younger. I guessed both were in their late twenties, one male and one female. Both were white, and all three were wearing black suits.

As we approached, the general said, "So sorry to keep you waiting. This is Scott Parker, the owner of this company."

Dad shook the three agents' hands and said, "These are my colleagues, John Thomas and Annie Hansen."

We all shook hands. "Nice to meet you all," the head agent said. "I'm Agent Murphy." He pointed to the young man and said, "This is Agent Carter." He then pointed at the woman and said, "This is Agent Taylor."

"I'm told you guys want to check out our new device that the president is interested in," Dad said.

"Yes. For security reasons," Agent Murphy said.

"I understand," Dad said. "If you will all follow me."

We all followed Dad to the third floor. Two soldiers stood at the elevator door, and another two stood in front of the lab entrance.

Dad walked in first, followed by the agents, the general, and then Annie and I filed in last. Gabby was already inside waiting for us. I assume she already met the agents because there were no introductions.

Dad went to the control computer and tapped on the keyboard. The screen lit up, and he entered the password I gave him. He then located a new hard drive and plugged it in.

I noticed all eyes were on Dad, so I took that opportunity to look for a pen and paper. I found both on a counter at the back of the room. I wrote a short note, folded the paper, and put it in my pocket.

"So, who wants to have their memories recorded?" Dad said.

Agent Murphy said, "You can do me."

"Okay," Dad said. "Lie on the machine face up."

Agent Murphy did as he was told and said, "Are you sure this is safe?"

"It's just like getting an MRI," Dad said.

"Okay, go ahead," he said.

Dad typed in a command and clicked a button. The machine started up. It went through the entire process, and when it was finished, Agent Murphy sat up, and Rafferty said, "How do you feel."

"I feel fine," he said. "It really is just like an MRI machine."

"So, are we okay with the president's visit?" Rafferty asked.

"Our people still have to finish checking the building, but I think it will be okay." Agent Murphy said.

"Very well then. We will let you get back to your work." Rafferty said.

Dad unplugged the hard drive, handed it to the agent, and said, "Here is a souvenir for you. It's better than photographs."

"Thanks. I guess I will never forget my time here," he said.

As everyone started filing out of the room, I took the folded paper out of my pocket, put it in my hand, and reached out to shake Agent Murphy's hand. I said, "Thank you, Agent Murphy. Let me know if I can help in any way."

When he felt the paper in his hand, he briefly looked surprised but recovered quickly, put his hand in his pocket, and said, "Thank you. I'll let you know if we need anything."

Annie and I stood by the door as everyone filed out. Gabby was last and gave me a dirty look as she passed but said nothing. I looked at Annie and shrugged.

We followed everyone downstairs, and eventually, the Secret Service people went off to do their own thing. Dad said, "I think that went well."

"We will see," Rafferty said.

"Well, I'm hungry," I said. "We should go get something to eat while we have time."

"No," said Rafferty. "I have this place locked down. We need to stay put until the president gets here. There's food in the break room."

"I wouldn't call that food," I said. I had no idea what was in the break room or even where the break room was, but I couldn't imagine we would find anything good there.

"It's that or nothing," Rafferty said.

"Okay. I guess it's better than nothing. Who else is hungry?" I said.

"I'm starving," Annie said.

"I could eat something," Dad said.

Rafferty and Gabby said nothing, so we wandered off toward the elevator. I whispered, "Who knows where the break room is?"

"It's on the second floor," Annie said. "I saw it listed when we looked for Parker's office."

We found the breakroom on the second floor and went inside. It was slightly bigger than Parker's office but wasn't a corner unit. The windows overlooked the main parking lot. To the left was a refrigerator, a microwave, a coffee maker, and a couple of cabinets above the counter and drawers below. There was also a vending machine with snacks in it. In the middle were two round tables with six chairs each, and to the right was a sofa with a coffee table and a large television.

I opened the refrigerator and saw several bottles of water and various condiments but no food. I took out three bottles of water and handed one to Annie and another to Dad. Dad checked the drawers, and Annie looked in the cabinets. There were a variety of plates, bowls, and utensils but no food.

"I guess our only choice is vending machine food," I said.

The machine accepted credit cards, so Dad put his card in and said, "What will it be?"

I remembered my promise to Annie and said, "You choose for me."

She got us each a granola bar and a bag of mixed nuts. Dad got crackers and cheese and a bag of popcorn. We sat down at one of our tables to enjoy our delicacy.

I said, "You guys should know I did something that might cause problems for us."

"What did you do?" Annie said.

"I slipped a note to the Secret Service guy."

"What did the note say?" Dad said.

"It said, 'The machine does more than you know. The president's life is in danger,'"

"If that works, he's going to be pissed," Dad said.

"I know," I said, "but I couldn't stand by and watch Parker steal the presidency."

Annie put her hand on my arm and said, "You did what you had to do. I'm proud of you."

I put my hand on hers and said, "Thanks, but I fear that I again put the people I love in harm's way."

"I became a cop because I wanted to help good people and stop bad people," Annie said. "I was always willing to risk my life for a noble cause, and saving the president and his wife from these psychopaths is the noblest cause I can think of."

"I'm proud of you, too," I said.

"I'm proud of both of you," Dad said, "but we need to plan what we will do if Rafferty turns on us."

"That could be difficult," I said. "He has an army backing him."

"Maybe," Annie said, "but this is America. A soldier is not likely to follow an order if he feels the person giving it is corrupt or compromised."

"I hope you are right," I said.

A few minutes later, I saw four identical black sedans driving away. We all watched as they passed the guard station one by one. Then the door opened, and Rafferty and Gabby walked in. Both were pointing pistols at us. I said, "Whoa, what is this all about?"

"I was just informed that the president decided to cancel his visit here today'" Rafferty said. "I was given no reason for the change of plans. One of you said something, and I want to know who."

"Just a minute," Dad said. "How dare you point guns at us over this. We worked just as hard as you to make this happen. How do you know an emergency didn't come up?"

"I don't know anything for sure, but I do know you three have not worked as hard as me on this. In fact, you all seem to have changed your mind about the plan," Rafferty said.

"No," I said. "We were all in agreement that the prudent thing would be to wait, but you foolishly plunged ahead without regard for consequences. You probably spooked them. I doubt we will get another chance because of your bullheadedness."

"That's bullshit," Gabby said. "I think you screwed up, Scott. I think these two were not converted. Tell me, pretty lady, how did Scott and I meet?"

Annie hesitated. She looked at me and then back at Gabby and said, "He picked you out of a lineup."

Gabby looked at Rafferty and said, "Just like I thought, Brian."

Rafferty pointed at me and said, "What about you? How did Gabby and I meet?"

"At Narcissists Anonymous," I said.

"How did you make such a blunder, Scott?" Rafferty said.

"I don't understand what happened," Dad said.

"We can fix this right now," Rafferty said.

They led us up to the lab on the third floor. We passed several soldiers, but none questioned why the general and his wife had us at gunpoint. When we got inside the lab, Rafferty instructed Dad to start up the machine. "Now, who wants to go first?" Rafferty said.

"Just get it over with," I said, walking toward the machine. As I passed Dad, I whispered, "Don't worry. Just do it."

Rafferty found the hard drive marked "Scott" and plugged it in.

I climbed onto the machine and said, "Okay, go ahead."

Annie screamed, "Noooo!" but Gabby shoved her gun hard into her temple.

Dad started up the program but hesitated to hit the start button. I nodded to him, and he clicked on the button. After the machine cycled through its process and shut down, I sat up, looked around the room, then held out my arms to look at them. "I need a mirror," I said.

Rafferty handed me a mirror, and after looking at my face, I said, "What the hell? Why am I in this body? What happened to the president?"

"It's a long story," Rafferty said. He then pointed at Annie, "You're next."

"No way," Annie said. "I'm not getting on that thing."

"You will get on it, or you will get a bullet in your brain," Gabby said.

"I would prefer that to being a psycho bitch like you," Annie said.

Gabby moved behind her, pressed her gun against Annie's back, and pulled her hair hard. "I would love to put you out of my misery right now," she said.

"Let me talk to her," I said.

"Not yet," Gabby said. "You still haven't told me how Scott and I met."

"That's a weird question," I said. "Why would you want to know that?"

Rafferty interrupted and said, "Sorry. You wouldn't know that Maryanne is Gabby now."

"What? Was Rafferty being difficult?"

"Yes, but that's not important right now," Gabby said. "Answer the question."

I said, "I was in Los Angeles on a business trip. You were the night manager at the hotel I stayed at. I told you that you were the prettiest night manager I ever saw, and we just hit it off after that."

"I guess the machine is working now," Gabby said. "Okay, go ahead and talk to her."

She backed away and stood by Rafferty's side, and I walked up to her and said loud enough for everyone to hear, "You have nothing to worry about. Once you do this, the two of us can be together forever." I then whispered, "I love your eyes and your boobs," and winked at her.

Her eyes opened wide, and I think she realized what happened. "Okay, fine," she said and got on the machine.

I removed Parker's hard drive and replaced it with Gabby's. I then motioned for Dad to start up the machine. He started up the program and hit the start button. The machine sprang to life, and the conveyor slowly pulled Annie's head into it. After several minutes it stopped, and Annie sat up. I handed her the mirror, and she looked at herself and said, "What is this? This is that cop woman. Why am I in her body?"

I said, "It's okay. I'll explain later."

Annie looked at me and then at Dad and said, "What is he doing here?"

"He's here because he's me now," Dad said, pretending to be Parker.

Annie stood up, and while everyone's eyes were on her, I reached up and collected the two syringes. I put one in my pocket and walked over to Annie. I put both hands in hers and said, "I am so glad to have you back." I rolled my eyes back toward Abbey, and she nodded that she understood.

Gabby and Rafferty had both put their guns away. I walked over to Rafferty while Annie made her way next to Gabby. I pointed at the machine and said, "We need to build more of these now."

I stressed the word "now," and Annie and I both injected our intended targets. Gabby and Rafferty both had shocked looks on their faces before dropping to the floor.

"What just happened?" Annie asked. "Why do I remember everything?

"Well," I said. "Remember I asked to record your memories? I recorded it on Gabby's hard drive and didn't change the label. So, the machine just replaced your memories with the same memories."

"I understand that," she said, "but I remember what happened after that. How is that possible?"

"I remember too," I said, "and I didn't expect that. If I were to guess, I would say that those new memories were in memory locations that didn't exist when our brains were scanned, so it didn't change them. That is probably why I remember some things from John's life because those memories were stored at a memory location that had no memories in Alex's brain."

Dad said, "I don't know what happened these last five years, but my original intention was to design a machine that only replaced memories that were different. That way, when a person's memories are lost, they could be restored without touching any of the other memories. If that is how the machine was designed, it would have seen that all the memories were identical, so it would have done nothing."

"This is all too crazy for me," Annie said. "Let's just say we were lucky."

"Sounds good to me," I said. "We were very lucky."

"By the way," Annie said, "how did you know how Parker and Gabriella met?"

"I did a little research. I was hoping to find something I could use against him. I never imagined that would be it."

"So, what should we do with these two? Annie asked.

"How would you feel about another Annie and John in this world?" I asked.

Chapter 27

Three months later, Annie and I stepped aboard a luxury yacht moored in Alex's hometown of Dunedin, Florida. Dad was standing on the deck with Bruno by his side. Bruno's tail started wagging when he saw us, and Dad said, "Welcome aboard, you two."

"Thanks for letting us use your boat, Dad," I said.

"I think you need to get used to calling me Scott," he said. "It would be awkward if someone overheard you."

Alex was also there with Lisa, who looked like she might have a baby at any moment. I knew her due date wasn't for a few more weeks, so I tried not to worry. "It's so good to see you two again," I said. "Where are the kids?"

"They are at home. My parents are there watching them," she said.

Lisa hugged Annie and said, "I don't know what we would have done without you guys. We are so happy you are here. You both look wonderful."

"Thank you," Annie said. "I can't tell you how happy we are to be here."

We went inside, where many people were standing around conversing. Most were dressed in casual Florida attire. Many had drinks in their hands. A small bar was set up on one end and a makeshift stage on the other. There were chairs and sofas crammed together along the perimeter so that the center space remained open.

Dr. Carr was the first to notice us, and she said, "Hello, Annie. Hello, John."

"Hello, Sarah," Annie said.

"We are happy you could come to Florida," I said.

"Who could resist a trip to Florida on a yacht?" she said.

"You came with Dad? I mean, you came with Scott?"

"Did he not tell you we are a thing now?"

"Must have slipped his mind, but I'm pleased he found a wonderful woman like you," I said.

"I'm happy for you, too," Annie said.

"You didn't know about Scott and Sarah?" came a voice from behind. I turned and saw the general and his wife.

"Brian. Maryanne. It's so good to see you. I didn't recognize you in that Hawaiian shirt and shorts, Brian."

"I hung up that uniform, as you know," Brian said.

"What you might not know is that Brian and I decided to take some time off and see the world," Maryanne said. "We figured Florida was a good place to start."

"That sounds like a lot of fun," Annie said. "What will you do when you return?"

"We thought maybe we would get into the dog training business since I do have experience with dogs," she said. "Part of the business would be teaching people how to handle their dogs, like a dog training school. The other part would be a non-profit dedicated to training and providing service dogs for vets. Do you know that a veteran with PTSD is three times less likely to commit suicide if they have a service dog?"

"I didn't know that," Annie said, "but I can certainly believe it's true."

"That sounds like a very worthwhile cause," I said. "I hope you guys have a wonderful trip, and best of luck to you in your new business."

"Thanks so much," Maryanne said. "By the way, we are happy to see Bruno is doing well."

"He never ceases to amaze me," Annie said. "He will be going back to work with me soon."

Just then, Annie's parents and her brother Michael approached us. Her mom hugged her and then me. Her dad hugged Annie and shook my hand. "It's good to see you again, John," he said.

"It's good to see you again, too, sir," I said.

"Bob," he said. "Call me Bob. I've told you that before."

Michael hugged Annie and shook my hand. "I guess I was wrong about you," he said. "You're a good man."

"Thank you, Michael," I said.

I saw my parents and waved at them. They came over, and I said, "Mom. Dad. Do you remember Annie's parents, Bob and Linda, and her brother, Michael?

"Sure, Mom said. "It's good to see you all again."

We then felt the boat start to move. We watched out the windows as it navigated out of the marina and into the intercostal waterway. After several minutes we made our way into the Gulf of Mexico. About fifteen minutes later, the boat stopped, and the engines shut down.

Scott got on the stage and picked up the microphone. He said, "Good evening, ladies and gentlemen. We are blessed to have every one of you on board today. As you know, it is a very special day. We are here to witness the wedding of my good friends, Annie Hansen and John Thomas. These two are very special to me. Some of you here know how special. Now, can I get the bride and groom, and the best man and maid of honor up on the stage?"

Annie and I stepped onto the stage. We were followed by Alex and Maryanne. The captain came out and took the microphone from Scott.

"As the captain of this beautiful yacht, it is my great pleasure and honor to be here today with Annette Hansen and Jonathan Thomas as they embark on their journey together as husband and wife.

Marriage is a promise, but it is much more than that. It is two hearts, two souls, two lives becoming one. It is a lifetime commitment to always be there for one another. It is a commitment to always give each other all the love you have, knowing it will come back to you in an endless cycle. Today, you, Annette, and you, Jonathan, will promise to support each other through all the ups and downs that life gives you, to laugh together, to cry together, to share in each other's joys and sorrows, and to grow old together.

Annie and John, your love for each other has brought you here today, and the love of family and friends has filled this place with people who want to share this special day with you. As you stand here together on this beautiful ocean, may the sea of life always be calm, and may your journey be filled with love, joy, and happiness.

Do you, Jonathan, take Annette to be your lawfully wedded wife, to have and to hold, through sickness and health, as long as you both shall live?"

"I do," I said.

"Do you, Annette, take Jonathan to be your lawfully wedded husband, to have and to hold, through sickness and health, as long as you both shall live?"

"I do," she said.

"And now, by the authority vested in me, I pronounce you husband and wife. Jonathan, now is a good time to kiss your bride."

Annie and I kissed, and the crowd erupted in cheers.

Two hours later, as the party started winding down and the boat was heading back to shore, Annie and I stood on the deck alone. She said, "I've wanted to tell you something important, but I was waiting for the perfect time. I think that time is now."

"Oh yeah? What do you want to tell me?" I asked.

"I'm pregnant."

About the Author

Charles Huss was born and raised in the suburbs of Chicago but has lived most of his adult life in the Tampa Bay area of Florida. He is a graduate of St. Petersburg College and is the writer of several blogs. He currently lives with his wife, Rose, and their three cats.

www.ingramcontent.com/pod-product-compliance
Lightning Source LLC
Chambersburg PA
CBHW050838180626
46814CB00007B/2512